THE ONLY ONE FOR ME

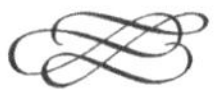

TONI JACKSON

CHAPTER 1

*S*ean Davenport reclined in the soft black leather chair that coordinated with his onyx desk. Dark red walls surrounded him in the quietly elegant space that served as the heart of his empire's operation. Afternoon sunlight streamed through the floor-to-ceiling windows, bathing the walls in a golden glow. Windows covered the length of the entire wall behind him, giving Sean a breathtaking view of the city he loved. There was a special connection for him here. The office and furniture had once belonged to his father.

When he assumed control, he left everything the same. Every day it reminded him of the struggle and sacrifices his father endured to build the company before his death.

A shrewd investor and businessman, Gregory Davenport worked eighty-hour weeks to establish Davenport Corporation. Sean and his mother, Elinor, often would not see him for days. No one was surprised when the stress caught up with Gregory. At forty-nine, his father died of a massive heart attack in his office, two months before Sean's twenty-fifth birthday.

A grim smile crossed Sean's face. His entire life his family, teachers, and even business associates, drove him to succeed. As the only child of Gregory Davenport, Sean grew up knowing he shouldered a heavy responsibility. He had been groomed his entire life to take over the legacy of Davenport Corporation.

When Sean turned nine, his father slowly began to involve him in the day-to-day operations of the company, while still allowing him to experience life on his own terms. He would bring Sean into the office for a few hours, before having him taken back home. There were days when other activities would prevent Sean from going to the office, but he always treasured the times he did. It was exciting, but in some ways, Sean felt he was visiting a stranger.

Sean's father lacked any real warmth. The only emotions he showed involved the company. He was consumed by the overwhelming need to leave something behind that would be remembered.

His father's death changed Sean's life. When he assumed control of the company, Sean slipped into his father's role with little effort. His expectations were higher…and the way he lived his life was a large part of the change. One of the things that stood out in Sean's mind was the need to keep the company in the family. He was an only child, as were both of his parents. For Sean, it was imperative that the Davenport name continue. He refused to let Gregory's legacy fall into the hands of strangers.

Unfortunately, one thing stood between Sean and the fulfillment of this expectation.

After years of preparing himself and building up The Davenport Corporation into one of the most powerful companies in the world, Sean discovered a peculiar irony. He carried a rare blood trait that could destroy his hopes and dreams.

Thanks to this condition, no woman could conceive his child…unless the woman carried the same or similar trait. The odds staggered Sean's mind.

"A one in seven million chance," the doctors told him regarding the probability of his compatibility success.

Good thing the son of Gregory Davenport never believed in the odds.

Lucky for him, being powerful, rich and determined had its benefits.

Sean placed his best private investigators and hackers on the path of determining the extremely small pool of women able to bear his child. Over the past few years, having an heir had become his obsession. There was no way would he let all of his hard work - and his father's - fall into the hands of some money-grubbing stranger upon his death.

Every day he left his house knowing there was a chance he might not make it to the job alive. The thought of it terrified him and kept him awake at night. He could barely wait until his team found his match. His preference was to have her as a surrogate. Although he wanted a child, the thought of a wife was a daunting one. All she had to do was agree to artificial insemination with Sean's sperm, adhere to strict specifications of diet, living conditions and any other methodology Sean deemed worthy of his unborn heir, and then deliver the child to him at birth, giving up all her parental rights to the child.

Seam found most people thought he was insensitive to believe a woman would be heartless enough to agree to such a plan. However, early in life Sean discovered the spellbinding power of money and its ability to assuage people's morality. Sean believed he could definitely win the woman's cooperation.

All he had to do was find her.

For the past two years, his investigators had worked

around the clock trying to locate someone compatible. Sean knew these things took time, but he was starting to get impatient. With all of the resources at his team's disposal, he knew that they should have discovered something by now. His frustration escalated with every negative result.

There was no use trying to concentrate on his paperwork. Sean's mind refused focus on the mundane while the search continued. Pushing away from the desk, he prepared to go into his first meeting of the day. Picking up his portfolio, he stepped away from the desk, then paused when his assistant informed him that Sam McKennon, his head investigator, was on the line.

Sean frowned. It was unusual for McKennon to call midmorning. The team usually delivered progress reports daily in the late afternoon. He took a deep breath, trying not to get his hopes up. But his mind still raced with possibilities as he hesitantly hit the intercom button to respond.

"Patch him through and tell my first meeting that I'll be in shortly."

Sean sat back down in his chair and took another deep breath. He noticed the slight tremor in his hand as he picked up the receiver.

"Davenport."

"Sean, this is McKennon." Sean pictured McKennon sitting in his office, his favorite size 13 cowboy boots propped on his desk and the Stetson hat he never removed, pushed back from his forehead. He reminded Sean of the detective McCloud from the old 70's television show.

McKennon worked for Sean's father for years, providing security. Now, he supervised Sean's physical and cyber security teams. He was one of the few people Sean trusted implicitly.

Sean picked up his pen and began tapping it on the desk. Feeling his heart rate increase, Sean took several more deep breaths, forcing himself to calm down. "You have news for me?"

There was a slight pause.

"We've found a match."

Although Sean had hoped for good news, he never expected to receive it. His pen dropped from his fingers. Now, just when he had almost given in and believed the doctors were right, his hard work seemed about to pay off.

"Where?" Sean asked.

The sound of papers shuffling traveled to him through the telephone. "Actually, right on the other side of town."

Closing his eyes, Sean fought to keep his voice steady. To think he had nearly given up when she was so close…

Sean's voice, when he spoke, echoed his disbelief. "You've been searching for two years, and when you finally manage to locate someone, they're right on the other side of town?" Sean's anger was evident in the hushed tone of his words.

McKennon, unfazed by Sean's anger, answered, "You have to understand, we weren't able to find her until we opened up the search. From your original criteria," McKennon paused hoping he would not have to mention the previous economic, racial, educational and taste preferences Sean had previously given the team. "There wasn't anyone. It wasn't until we expanded the search that we found someone. It wasn't like we could just go pick someone off the shelf."

Sean stayed silent as he waited for McKennon to finish. He took the time to pull himself together. It was hard to believe that after so much time, he was on the verge of achieving his goal. "So who is she?"

"She's an up and coming artist by the name of Danielle Knox. Does sculptures. Seems to be doing pretty well for herself. Getting lots of recognition for her work."

Sitting forward, Sean's mind was already working ahead

to his next step. "Do you think she would be willing to go along with my plans?"

McKennon hesitated again before replying. "In all honesty? No."

Sean frowned and sat straighter in his chair. "Why not?"

"I'll send the files we have on her and you can judge for yourself. We've interviewed a few people about her. Their statements are in the file. Ms. Knox seems determined to do things on her own, without the interference of other people's ideas and manipulations to steer her off her own course. Seems that there have been benefactors that have offered to help her set up studios, teach, whatever she wanted to do."

"She's that talented?" Sean's mind raced. Maybe he could use her ambition to his advantage. Someone who fully vested in their career would not want to have the responsibility of a child, would they? If he was careful, this could work to his advantage.

"I don't know anything about art, but even I like the pieces I've seen." Coming from a rough and rugged man like McKennon, that was saying a lot.

Sean thought about his next course of action. "Send me the information - including all of her medical records."

"They're on their way."

"Oh, and McKennon," Sean asked, "Are there pictures?"

"Yeah. She's a pretty little thing," McKennon laughed. "Not your usual type though."

Sean wondered what he meant.

CHAPTER 2

*T*he folder containing the woman's information was waiting on Sean's desk when he returned from his meeting that afternoon. He flipped through the report, carefully scanning the details, determined not to miss anything. Anyone seeing him would think that he was planning a company takeover. In some ways, he was. He absorbed every detail, from her favorite color to the type of soap she used. The more he read, the more he realized that McKennon was right. This woman, Danielle Knox, was not the type to act as a surrogate for money.

Her father, Daniel Knox, had died in a car accident when she was a baby. Her mother, Katherine, an only child, and Danielle's maternal grandfather, Colby, raised her. Both of them died just before Danielle's eighteenth birthday. There were no cousins or other relatives around, much like himself. Danielle was alone in the world. Still, everything Sean's team discovered said that this woman had a strong sense of independence.

The next page of the report detailed her life after high school. Danielle attended the D'Allonge école d'art school in

New York for several years. The report listed several relationships since then, but evidently, none that made her take things to the next level, since according to her medical records she was still a virgin. Sean took the time to digest all of this information as he reached over for the envelope of photos that he had saved until last. He paused, afraid of what he might find.

What if she looked like a Saint Bernard?

Instead, Sean found himself relieved and very surprised.

Smiling for the first time since he started his personal mission, he decided McKennon was right. Danielle Knox was not his usual type.

However, she was still beautiful.

He thought of the models, debutantes, and actresses that were his usual dates. Sean never cared for any of them. They were the eye candy expected on the arm of someone rich and famous. Tall, svelte women who looked like they never ate anything but carrot sticks and water. It struck Sean as funny that he had never considered that the woman they found would not be white. He had never even realized it until this particular moment of staring into the face of an exquisite brown-skinned black woman.

Sean knew that there were still some that would frown on a prominent white businessman having a relationship with a black woman. As far as Sean was concerned, anyone's issues with the possibility of the relationship were their own. They may have an issue with it, but the Davenport Corporation held a strong enough position in the business world to survive it. They could accept his choice, or he could ruin them.

It was that simple.

Sean never had an issue of dating outside his race; he had just never found a woman - black or otherwise - who made him want to take things to the next level. Danielle Knox's picture made him visualize the future. Family and children, definitely more than one.

According to the records, she was twenty-eight, five-four, one hundred and twenty-five pounds. The pictures included in the package showed a petite woman with flawless dark brown skin and long, dark hair braided into a ponytail and that hung down past her shoulders.

As Sean studied her picture, he had the urge to see if Danielle's skin was as soft as it looked. His only disappointment with the report was the inability to tell much about her figure from the photos.

Placing the pictures aside, Sean turned back to the file. A notation on the side of one document stated that Danielle's gallery was hosting an invitation-only showing downtown on September twenty-first. Looking over at his calendar, Sean realized the date was only three days away. Making a mental note to attend, he realized that this would be a perfect opportunity for him to meet Danielle and make a decision about how he wanted to proceed.

Sean continued reading, making sure he did not miss any pertinent details. It was not until he was looking through her medical records that he paused. His eyes narrowed as he did some mental calculations and smiled. If he was careful, everything might work out to his advantage after all.

Opening his briefcase, he slid the file inside and snapped it closed. His mind was already working out details as he exited his office and stopped by his assistant's desk.

Ms. Davis was nothing if not efficient. Her desk was spotless except for two trays that contained incoming and outgoing correspondence. She looked up at her boss and smiled when he stopped at her desk.

"Yes, Mr. Davenport?"

"I'm leaving for the day, Ms. Davis. I need one invitation

to the Visions Gallery Piedmont for their showing on Friday night."

"Yes, sir," she answered. A pen and pad magically appeared on her desk, her pen making scratching noises on the notepad as her employer watched her take notes.

"If anything major happens, I'll be available on my cell phone."

"Yes, sir," Ms. Davis answered, nodding. Sean said good night and walked towards the elevator. Knowing Ms. Davis, he would have the invitation by morning.

Sean decided to plot his strategy tonight. If this was going to work, there were plans that he needed to put into place. He could not afford to have anything go wrong.

CHAPTER 3

Sunlight streamed through the windows into the small workshop Danielle had created in her garage, highlighting the particles of dust floating through the air. Danielle had the garage closed in, with a door leading to the driveway. It helped that it was an attached garage. A contractor managed to run vents through to the workshop from the house to give her heating and air conditioning, as well as improved ventilation.

Sounds of a hammer tapping lightly against a chisel echoed throughout the room over the soft rhythm of R&B pouring from the radio. Danielle's fierce expression spoke to her concentration. The painstaking definition of every curve and line of her sculptures was Danielle's signature, gaining her work greater and greater recognition by critics of her field. Completely engrossed in her work, Danielle missed hearing her friend and manager, Clayton Thomas walk into the room.

"Hey, Dani baby!" Dani took a moment to finish the curving shoulder she had been outlining before looking up.

Taking a deep breath, she felt relieved that this piece was almost finished. After two months straight working on sculptures for her show, she was more than ready for a break.

"Hi, Clayton." Dani smiled at the picture he presented standing in her dusty workshop. Clayton was dressed head to toe in his standard somber black, making his olive complexion seem paler. He was being his usual melodramatic self, walking around the sculpture, not saying a word. Dani smiled at his attempts to look like a serious art critic. The only thing missing was a black tam cocked to the side and pencil-thin mustache etched on his thin face.

Clayton stopped, hands on his hips. "Not bad, not bad at all."

"Thanks." She smirked. One thing Dani never had to worry about was Clayton inflating her ego. Her closest friend in art school, Clayton had repeatedly proven that he had an eye for art. When they had graduated, Clayton came back and started a gallery. Clayton never spoke of how he acquired the money, and Dani never asked. Any kind of financial talk sailed over her head; she never understood how those matters worked. Paying bills on time flustered Dani. If not for her automatic bill payer, she would be in trouble. Clayton commissioned and displayed other artists to pay the ongoing bills of running a decent gallery, but his main goal had always been to support - and when necessary, push - Dani's artistic talent.

She was going to be a star…Clayton could sense it.

Clayton raised an eyebrow at his best friend. As usual, Dani's work inspired his business side. "Will you be finished with this one by tomorrow evening?" he asked.

"It's possible," Dani shrugged. "If you promise to let me work all day tomorrow - undisturbed."

Clayton frowned. He had created quite a buzz around the

showing he'd scheduled for Dani's work the next day at his gallery. He zeroed in on his friend trying to fudge on the primping-time he knew she needed to get herself physically presentable to the art-buying public. "Dani, you know if I don't hound you about getting dressed early, you'll come to your own showing all dusty and dirty." Clayton flailed his hands around for emphasis.

Dani knew he was right. Dressing up and mingling with people was not one of her strong points. Her love was creating art, molding and shaping things. She belonged in the studio…not chitchatting at cocktail parties. So far, she managed to get out of the shows, which had created an air of mystery about her, but Clayton insisted she attend this one.

Her face took on an innocent expression. She loved teasing Clayton. When it came to art shows at his gallery, he was more of a perfectionist than Dani.

"Well that about answers your question then doesn't it?" said Dani.

"You can be such a bitch sometimes," Clayton said moodily as he crossed his arms and stared at her.

"I know," she said smiling. "Isn't it wonderful?"

Clayton rolled his eyes and moved to drape himself across the small that couch Dani kept in her work area in case exhaustion drove her to take a much needed a nap.

"Anyway," Clayton said after he got comfortable, "guess whose office just contacted me for an invitation to come to the showing?"

"Whose?" Dani asked absently as she began sanding down the chisel marks on the statue. Her mind was already back on her work.

"Sean Davenport!" Clayton squealed, clapping his hands, barely able to control himself. Dani looked at him blankly. The name didn't ring a bell.

Clayton sobered.

Dani looked confused. "Who's Sean Davenport? An art critic?" She frowned. Dani left it to Clayton to keep track of the critics. They were worse than little kids with their temper tantrums; Dani didn't have the time or patience for them.

Clayton shook his head and sank back against the couch. "God girl, we have got to get you out more! Sean Davenport, of Davenport Corporation?"

Dani shrugged and turned back to the statue. "Sorry, the name means nothing to me."

"Genre Technology? Baker's Dozen? None of this rings a bell?" Clayton crossed his arms and used one perfectly manicured finger to tap on his lip. "On second thought, that might work in our favor. If you don't know anything about him, then you have no cause to be nervous when he shows up. Works for me!" Clayton jumped up. Danielle marveled at the amount of energy Clayton exhibited before a showing.

"I've got to run past the gallery and make sure Tina has everything in place for tomorrow night."

Dani laughed. "You know she's still pissed that you're making her work the coat check."

Clayton waved his hands at her. "She'll be all right. That'll keep her out of trouble. Last time after she cornered poor Mr. Gleason and his wife came after her….that was not pretty." He started for the door then turned.

"And…don't forget to bring those insurance papers with you when you come this evening."

Frowning, Dani crossed her arms. "I still don't understand why you need a policy on me. Isn't it enough to insure my work?"

"Sweetie, if Tina Turner's legs can be insured for a mill, then so can you. It's just a precautionary measure."

"Fine." Dani rolled her eyes.

"I'm serious. You and Tina's legs, Dani," Clayton called out to her as he walked out the door.

Dani laughed and waved.

Glancing at her watch, Dani looked back at the statue. "Maybe I have time to sneak off for a new dress since some big shot's coming," she muttered.

Dani put her tools on a small tripod table near her sculpture. She closed the studio door behind her and went into the house for a quick shower. As the water pelted down on her, she wondered about Sean Davenport. What type of person was he? Dani's contact with the privileged set was limited to what she read in magazines. And, since she only read art magazines, her world was very limited.

Although it was tempting to stay in the shower until all of the hot water ran out, Dani cut her shower short and stepped out to dry off. She grabbed underclothes and her standard uniform of jeans and a T-shirt. Sticking her feet into a pair of tennis shoes, she glanced at her watch to see how much time she had left.

Good, she had at least three hours to find a dress before the mall closed. Taking a deep breath, Dani grabbed her jacket and car keys.

"All right, here goes nothing," Dani mumbled to herself. She drove over to the nearest mall in the hopes of finding something appropriate to wear. Clayton would kill her if he knew she had not taken the time to get her dress yet.

Clayton had staged small showings before, but nothing the size of this one. Dani knew he wanted everything to go perfectly and was doing her best to do her part. Even though the last thing she wanted was to dress up and go out.

Dani stepped out of the car, walked inside the mall and cringed. Shopping was not her strong point. After walking around lost for twenty minutes, she spotted a store on the second level displaying slinky, sexy dresses in the window. Feeling bold, she headed in that direction, only to find her hopes crushed as she began to check the price tags. Good God, they were expensive! She ran into the same problem, store after store.

"There's not enough fabric here to be three hundred dollars," Dani muttered as she handled one dress that could have fit a three-year-old. Dani was about to give up and go back home when she noticed a small boutique tucked away in the corner of the second level. Strolling through the shop, a simple black dress at the back of the store drew her attention.

A saleswoman emerged, seemingly from nowhere, in a beautiful floor length multicolor dress. The woman reminded Dani of the gypsies she had seen in movies when she was younger.

"You could really do this justice with your shape," the woman said, taking the dress from the rack.

Dani eyed the dress with a dubious look. "You think so?" She had always been self-conscience of her generous curves.

"Oh yes. I should know. I made it." The woman's smile brightened at the expression on Dani's face.

"You're kidding." Dani looked at her in disbelief.

The saleswoman shook her head. "Here, go try it on."

Dani's hands itched to grab the dress, but she drew back. "I would, but...I'm on a tight budget and I don't see the price tag."

The woman just smiled and held the dress out towards Dani again. "Don't worry about that. Just try it on."

Dani took the dress into the fitting room and put it on. She was amazed by how well it fit. It could have been made for her. She stepped out of the dressing room to model it.

"See?" said the woman, beaming. "I told you it would fit perfectly."

"Okay." Dani turned to look at her, grimacing. "Now what's the punch line?"

"No punch line," the saleswoman said, then named a price that had Dani's eyebrows rising.

"That's all?" Dani asked in amazement. "No catches?"

The woman smiled at her while shaking her head.

"What are we waiting for then? I'll meet you at the register!" Dani tossed her hair over her shoulder as she went to take the dress off.

When Dani got home an hour later, she was exhausted, but happy. She took one of the two-inch heeled pumps she had just purchased with all the money she saved from the dress, out of the box and sighed. After all this, this guy had damned sure better buy something.

Dani laid the dress across the old faded armchair in her bedroom, then turned and looked at her hair. Oh, God! When was the last time she had gotten it done? At least three months, she guessed glancing at her split ends.

Dani's quasi-hair stylist, Shelia, came to mind. Dani did not frequent the shop enough to consider herself a REAL client, but because the two women got along well, Shelia always made room for Dani. Dani dialed and prayed that Sheila had not left the shop to go to Bingo, one of her favorite pastimes. She was light-headed with relief when Sheila answered. After promising to create a small Afrocentric statue for the front of Sheila's shop, Sheila agreed to come into the shop before normal hours the next morning to style Dani's hair. A satisfied smile spread across Dani's face as she ticked off another item on her checklist for tomorrow evening's gala.

Dani glanced toward the studio, wanting to go back to work. However, if she was going to make it to the hairdresser's on time in the morning, she needed to get some sleep. After debating for a minute, she headed towards the studio to finish the last stages of her sculpture. She could always sleep under the hair dryer at the salon.

Sometime around two a.m. Dani made her way into her bedroom, exhausted.

CHAPTER 4

Sean walked into the gallery Friday night, surprised to discover a rather large crowd milling around several sculptures. Impressed, he surveyed the room. His eyes paused on a show-stopping statue whose long smooth lines gleamed with life. As a rule, he did not go for the modern styles that passed as art these days, but something in this particular piece called out to him. Maybe it was the fact that the woman in the sculpture held a child close to her breast.

The piece symbolized everything Sean wanted.

A mother and a child.

A family to make everything complete.

A child that he could groom and set in place to take over his legacy.

If he stared at it long enough, he could picture the face of the woman that would bear his child, her arms cradling…his legacy.

Out of the corner of his eye, Sean noticed a slim man dressed all in black walking towards him. The man was so slight, Sean could imagine the lightest breeze carrying him away.

Stopping in front of Sean, the man held out his hand before speaking.

"Hi, I'm Clayton Thomas. Sean Davenport, right?"

"Right." Sean nodded and clasped the stranger's hand. The frail man's grip surprised Sean, causing him to change his first assessment of Clayton as a dismissible PR agent. A quiet strength resonated from Clayton, whose eyes were clear and direct.

"Well, thanks for coming and welcome to my gallery," said Clayton.

Sean watched Clayton's expression shift when he observed Sean's interest in the statue.

"I could not help but notice that this piece has captured your attention. It's one of my favorite works, also. We call it The Madonna.

Sean studied the sculpture. Clayton had wisely positioned it under a soft light, giving it an otherworldly appearance.

"How much does something like this go for?" Sean asked. The question about the price was a distraction. Sean had already decided to buy it.

"This one is ten thousand." Clayton shrugged at Sean's raised eyebrow. "Granted, it's a little steep for a first show-ing, but there's just something about it that seems to draw a person in." Clayton motioned towards the other statues strategically positioned in the room. "Would you like to view some of the other items?"

Sean shook his head and smiled. "No. I want this one." Reaching into his pocket, Sean pulled out his wallet. Clay-ton's eyes brightened considerably when he recognized the platinum credit card between Sean's fingers. "Put it on this and have it delivered to my house," Sean said smiling.

"Certainly, Mr. Davenport,"

Clay nodded, gleefully waving the card. "I'll be right back."

Normally, Sean left art purchases to his operations manager. However, he intended to have this statue occupy a special place in his home.

Sean watched as Clayton tried to look casual working his way across the room, when his body language showed he wanted to run to the scan the card. Sean scrutinized Clayton as he paused to talk to a beautiful brown-skinned woman who stood surrounded by a small crowd. Dressed in a sleeveless black dress that left little to his imagination, Sean let his mind drift free with possibilities.

Every curve of her body was defined and outlined by the black dress; it was more sensual to Sean than seeing her completely naked. His body tightened. He wanted to slide the silky material slowly down her body. As she turned around to face him, Sean was surprised to see the woman from the photos.

Danielle Knox.

Sean's eyes locked with hers as she smiled and walked towards him. He took his time studying her. Jet-black hair fell below her shoulders in casual curls that framed her face. The front of her dress scooped low, revealing the tops of the firm, full swell of her breasts. The rest of the dress emphasized her flat stomach and her gently flaring hips, with a slight teasing flare at the bottom.

His breath caught in his throat when Danielle, during a slight interruption, turned to speak to someone behind her. It was then that he noticed the dress had no back. Danielle's delicious chocolate skin lay exposed. The slinky fabric did not pick back up until it caressed her tiny waist and ample thighs just before draping to the back of her thighs.

Danielle's pictures, though beautiful, were a complete contrast to the sexy woman before him.

Sean's sexual interest sped past aroused and straight to possession. He wondered what Danielle wore beneath the dress—if anything. When she turned towards Sean again, he continued his open perusal, wondering how well they would fit together. Sean calculated that without heels, Danielle's head would just reach his shoulder.

Their eyes locked as Danielle finally reached him. She stopped a few inches away and smiled broadly. The subtle cologne she wore caressed his senses and lured him closer.

"Clayton couldn't wait to tell me that you'd purchased one of my pieces. Thank you. I'm Dani Knox," she said. Sean's body jumped in response to her deep, husky-toned voice.

Sean took the hand she extended to him and felt a jolt of electricity race through his anatomy. He just stopped himself from wrapping his arms around her and pulling her flush against his body. Instead, he lifted her hand to his lips and kissed the soft skin inside her wrist.

"Sean Davenport. It's beautiful. Like its' creator."

A delicate blush spread across Dani's cheeks that only managed to increase her beauty. "Thank you, again." An impish grin appeared on her face. "Since you seem to be in the mood to spend, can I show you some of my other works?"

"What I'd really like," Sean said moving closer to whisper in Dani's ear, "is to take you to a late supper."

He was disappointed when Dani stepped back, her smile dimming. "I don't know. Clayton made me promise to mix and mingle for a couple of hours before disappearing." A hint of her smile teased him. "Even though a late supper does sound nice."

At that moment, Clayton breezed up to hand Sean his receipt just as Dani finished speaking. He stage whispered, "Girlfriend, this guy just dropped ten grand for your sculpture within five minutes of walking in the door. The least you can do is have a late supper with him."

Dani rolled her eyes at Clayton before stage whispering back. "You're such a tramp."

"Go." Clayton waved her away. "Enjoy yourself. You deserve it." Clayton turned and walked back down into the crowd after proudly placing a sold tag on the Madonna statue. Dani turned back to Sean laughing.

"I guess I've been given permission to leave. Let me go and get my coat."

Sean watched Dani's hips swing back and forth as she walked away towards the coat check. Danielle Knox had turned out to be a very intriguing woman. Sweet and seductive instead of a calculating Barbie doll; the type Sean knew all too well. How refreshing.

As Dani approached the coat check, he noticed a redhead staring past the artist to check him out. She was very attractive, but for some reason she did not capture his attention like Dani. Sean had a feeling he was going to enjoy this night very, very much.

CHAPTER 5

*D*ani felt the heat of Sean's gaze as she walked over to the coat check where her best friend, Tina Diaz, was working. Tina's long dark red curls were pulled back off her face in an attempt to make the sexy woman look innocent and professional. Unfortunately, it was not working. All night men had been trying to find excuses to go to the coat check and try their luck at asking her out.

Men loved Tina's full, pouty lips and hot, sexy Latin looks. Her dark, smoky eyes and curvaceous figure never failed to attract attention. The biggest contrast in her appearance was the red hair she inherited from her Irish grandfather. The combination stopped men in their tracks.

Noticing Tina straining to check out Sean, Dani smirked.

Tina's eyes narrowed as she looked at the smirk on Dani's face. "Girl, who's that?" she said, nodding to where Sean stood waiting.

"That, my dear friend," Dani took a moment to glance back at Sean flirtatiously, "is the infamous Sean Davenport that Clayton was going crazy about."

Tina's eyes widened. "Of Davenport Corporation? Multimillion dollar tycoon? One of the most ruthless businessmen to ever walk the face of the earth?" Her friend was suddenly on the alert. One thing Tina knew was men. Especially rich men.

Dani laughed. "I don't know about all that. I just know he bought the Madonna."

"The Madonna? Whew! So what's he doing on this side of town?"

Dani wondered the same thing when Clayton told her Sean Davenport was coming to the show. For the amount of money this man made in a day, he could have been at some exclusive event where the patrons were served thousand dollar bottles of champagne while some anorexic size two blond in skyscraper heels fawned over him. Not here, where a few lukewarm bottles of Chardonnay and some meat and cheese platters from the local deli were the most they could offer for hors d'oeuvres. Tina asked a question and pulled her from her reverie. "Is he slumming?" she asked.

"Don't know, don't care," answered Dani. She shrugged. "I just know that the house note is paid for the next six months."

Tina rested her cheek on her hand while she checked Sean out. "He is a sexy beast though, isn't he?"

Dani turned to look at Sean. He was patiently watching them from the lobby. It was difficult to tell what was running through his mind. His expression gave nothing away.

"Probably knows it, too." Dani glanced down at her nails. "He wants me to have a late supper with him."

Eyes wide, Tina's voice dropped to a whisper. "Seriously?" She took a moment to pat her perfectly styled hair as a grin spread across her face. "Girl, I'd have a late supper with him all right. And a late breakfast."

Laughter bubbled up inside of Dani. Anyone listening to their conversation would think Tina was loose. Only Dani knew Tina was extremely discriminating in who she dated. Tina just liked teasing Dani because she had no real experience with men. Dani shook her head. "Not on the first date. Maybe not for the next several dates."

"You've got to take the opportunities where you can, girl." Tina propped her hand on her hip.

"Hmm…like you did with Mr. Johnston at that last showing," Dani teased. "You're lucky you got out of here in one piece."

"That wasn't my fault." Tina pouted her lips. "He was trying to feel me up on the sly. When I called his bluff and his wife saw him, he tried to fake amnesia." Both women laughed at the memory. The man felt so guilty at the scene his wife started, he bought four paintings that were being shown and left as fast as he could.

Tina shrugged. "Anyway, I still say you're crazy. The way they say he goes through women, you'd better get it on the first date. There may not be another. What have you got to lose? Wouldn't you want your first time to be with somebody who knows what they're doing?"

"And how do we know that for sure?" Dani shook her head at her friend and held out her hand. "Girl, give me my coat and let me get out of here."

"All right. But I'm telling you, you aren't getting any younger. You need to brush out those cobwebs out and take the plunge."

Dani turned towards Sean where he still waited patiently near the statue. The intensity of his focus made her feel like she was his prey.

"Bye, Tina. I'll call you tomorrow," Dani murmured and walked away.

CHAPTER 6

As Dani walked back over to Sean, she admired his chiseled features, his deep green eyes, and the way his dark hair curled over his forehead. His skin held only the slightest tan, telling Dani that he spent most of his time indoors. Sean's body was no slouch either. Her mind began to wander, imagining what he would look like without those clothes. The look in his eyes as she drew closer made her feel like the sexiest woman in the world.

His body looked solid. The fit of his pullover hinted at a lean, muscular body kept in the best of shape. A few dark hairs dusted the part of his chest that was visible. Too bad he wore loose slacks; she would love to see if he had a nice tight ass to go with the rest of him.

"I'm ready." Dani smiled up at Sean.

"Good." The hand he placed at the small of her back warmed her through the coat and dress she wore. Dani refrained from leaning back against his body as he escorted her out of the door and signaled to the valet to get his car.

'This should be interesting,' she thought as she stole a quick glance at him. Dani was not surprised to see the valet pull up in a black BMW and hand Sean the keys. He smoothly tipped the valet and walked over to open the door for her. Although Dani had dated several men of different races, she never found herself particularly attracted to white men. Until now. Sean Davenport appealed to all of her senses.

She slid inside, loving the feel of the soft leather seats. This was a long way from her beat up Stanza that rattled up and down the street. Smiling, she snuggled into the seat. So… this was how the other half lived. With any luck, she could make enough to buy one of these for herself.

Sean got in and smiled at her before pulling away from the curb.

Being around him was comfortable, contrary to how she thought she would feel.

He waited a few minutes before breaking the silence. "So how long have you been an artist?"

Dani smiled. "As long as I can remember, I've been creating things. It was all I ever wanted to do."

"Did you always sculpt? Or do you also paint?"

She shook her head. "No. Of course in school, they're not exactly going to give you a hammer and chisel and let you have your way." She smiled. "So….while I was at school, I was a good little girl with my paints and clay, and when I got home, I whipped out my knives and hammers."

Sean laughed. The deep, husky sound sent a chill through her body.

"Sounds like you were not the one to play with on dates," said Sean.

"No. I wasn't," Dani said. "But I didn't go out a lot. I would get so involved with my sculptures that I would lose track of time and forget about my dates. Eventually, people just stopped asking."

Dani turned to him. "And what about you? Everyone

refers to you as THE corporate shark. How much of that is true?"

"Shark?" he frowned. "I wouldn't call myself a shark. Just determined. When I see something I want, I go after it." He gave Dani a look that shot a bolt of heat through her body.

She smiled. "Oh really?"

Sean stopped at the upcoming red light and turned to study her. "Yes, really. It's not worth having if it's not worth fighting for."

The intensity of his stare caught her off guard. Blushing, she turned towards the passenger window when the light changed. The rest of the ride passed in silence, something intangible floating in the air between them.

Sean took them to an intimate restaurant downtown that she had passed, but never had the opportunity to patronize. A valet rushed forward and Sean walked around to help her out of the car. She was surprised when he took her hand and curled it around his arm. She was a little nervous strolling into the restaurant with him. This was not her world. It was his. Looking at the well-dressed people seated at the tables, she resisted the urge to turn and run.

They had barely stepped into the restaurant when the maître d' recognized Sean and scrambled to greet the tycoon. "Welcome, Mr. Davenport. Your usual table is available."

Sean nodded. "That would be fine, Christophe."

Christophe led them up a discrete set of stairs on the side of the restaurant that led to a private dining room. As they stepped inside, Dani saw a single table set with candles and two place settings. She smirked at Sean after the door closed. "This is your usual table? A private dining room?"

He shrugged. "It's difficult to enjoy your food when people are gawking and stopping by your table all the time. They never seem to understand that I'm here to eat just like they are."

"I can understand that. Never had it happen," she laughed. "But I can understand."

Sean grinned and helped her into her chair. "If you keep creating sculptures like the one I purchased tonight, you will. Trust me."

"Maybe, but it's not about the money. The money's never been that important to me."

"Really?" Sean leaned forward. "Why not? You have to admit, money is rather handy for solving problems."

"True," Dani agreed. "But sometimes it creates others."

Sean studied her closely, seeing the sincerity in her comment. It took him a minute to gather his thoughts, but before he could open his mouth to speak, the waiter approached.

"Would you like your usual wine selection, sir?"

He turned to Dani. "Do you have any wine preferences?"

"No." Dani shook her head. "I'm not much of a drinker."

"Ahh. Well, you have to have a drink tonight. To celebrate." He turned back to the waiter. "Bring my usual selection and the menu, and then give us fifteen minutes before returning."

"Yes, Mr. Davenport." The waiter hurried away, only to return two minutes later with an open bottle of Chardonnay, two glasses, and the menus before scurrying away once again.

"You have them well trained I see." Dani tried to hold in her laughter at the sight of the waiter almost tripping over his feet to serve Sean.

Sean felt something in him shift as he watched the hint of laughter in Dani's eyes. She was so refreshing and so different from the women in his past. He leaned back and smiled - his first real smile of the evening. "It helps when you own the restaurant."

Her eyes widened in shock. Then her laughter bubbled over. "I guess it would."

"So tell me," Dani asked. "Do you always travel alone? I thought people of a certain… um… salary range usually had some kind of security with them at all times?"

"I value my privacy. There are trackers on my cars and the GPS on my phone is monitored. I'm followed, but they stay out of sight. Do you know how uncomfortable it is to have an intimate conversation when there are big, burly, gun toting men hanging on to your every word?" Dani began laughing uncontrollably.

Sean kept her laughing with funny anecdotes and stories, keeping her wineglass filled throughout the meal until she had to put her hand over the glass to stop him.

"Enough," she said, holding up her other hand. "My head is swimming. I don't even know how I'm going to make it through the restaurant without embarrassing myself."

"Don't worry about that. The restaurant closed thirty minutes ago."

CHAPTER 7

"What! So you mean we're holding people up from going home?" Dani eased up from the table by holding onto the back of the chair. Although a little woozy, she managed to stay upright without any assistance.

"It's okay," Sean said holding up his hand. "It takes them at least this long to shut down for the night." Dani felt a little better about the situation, but not by much.

It helped that she was relaxed. Dani very seldom drank and tonight she had gone past her one drink limit.

Trying his best to hide his smile, Sean stood up and walked over to the tipsy, yet charming sculptor, and wrapped his arms around her, pulling her close to his body. He enjoyed having her in his arms. He loved the way her body felt next to his.

Dani stiffened. Even though she found Sean attractive, she was not used to having men she just met treat her with such familiarity. Taking a deep breath, she chided herself for being such a prude. Instead, she tried to concentrate on the feeling of being in Sean's embrace. He was, after all, very rich, and quite good-looking. It was not every day that a girl could have a fling with a rich playboy. After a few minutes, she began to relax as his cologne wafted around her; masculine but not overpowering.

"Come on, it's okay. Relax against me," Sean crooned. He held Dani close and led her towards the end of the hall to an elevator. "This will take us downstairs to my car."

Dani continued to lean against him once they stepped into the elevator.

"Are you okay to drive?" she asked on the elevator ride down, frowning.

"Trust me, I'm fine." The doors opened to reveal a well-lit garage, with Sean's car parked a few steps away.

While they were having dinner, the temperature outside had dropped a few degrees. The chill in the air helped to sober Dani, helping to clear her thoughts. Glancing over her shoulder, Dani admired the masculine image Sean presented standing behind her. "Maybe I could stay at a room down here somewhere so you wouldn't have to drive me all the way back to the other side of town. I could catch a cab back in the morning." The expression on Sean's face told her he was not in agreement with her suggestion.

"Would that be any kind of way to treat a date?" Sean responded by leading Dani over to his car. "If you really wanted to be helpful, you could stay with me tonight. My house is only a few blocks away."

Dani heard a chirp of the alarm on Sean's car as it disengaged, and the doors unlocked. She leaned against the side of the car while he opened the door for her and helped her inside.

Easing into the car and relaxing against the buttery leather Dani smiled. "Tina would just love this," she mumbled as Sean closed her door and walked around to the other side of the car.

"Who's Tina?" he asked, sliding behind the steering wheel.

"My best friend," Dani answered. Her lips curved into a smile as her eyes traveled the length of his body. "She said I should sleep with you tonight and not worry about the consequences."

Sean fought to hold back his grin. "So why don't you take her advice?" He reached for Dani's left hand, his thumbs stroking circles over her palm. Just that small touch made her think of decadent things, like his fingers rubbing circles all over her body.

The remaining wine coursing through Dani's body loosened her tongue and gave her the courage to say what was on her mind.

"Sleep with you?" she giggled. "It's tempting." Dani rolled her head on the headrest to face Sean. "You are a sexy little green-eyed devil. However, I don't think that's a good idea. If I knew you better..."

Sean cut her off. "I understand. At least let me treat you to a special surprise."

Dani lifted her head from its comfortable position. "What kind of surprise?"

Sean smiled at her. "It wouldn't be a surprise if I told you, now would it?"

Pouting, Dani debated about what the surprise could be. They had talked a lot during dinner, but he gave no sign that there was anything else in store for the evening.

"Dani?" Sean whispered and leaned over, his face just inches from hers.

"Hmm?" She blinked her eyes to see his face so close to hers. "What are you doing?" she whispered.

"Convincing you." Pressing his lips against hers, Sean captured Dani's mouth until she responded. Sean's hands slid through Dani's hair and cupped the back of her head as he took the kiss to another level, sliding his tongue inside her mouth. After what seemed like forever, he reluctantly pulled away.

That one kiss made Dani want to give Sean anything he wanted. "You are so bad," she groaned.

"I try to be." He whispered, smiling. Sean could not remember the last time he had enjoyed himself this much with any woman, much less one he purposely set out to seduce. "Come with me," he whispered. "I have the perfect ending to the evening."

"I must be crazy." Dani closed her eyes again and was silent for a moment. A debate waged inside her. For years, she had saved herself for the man she would marry, and for what? Here she was on the edge of thirty with no husband in sight. No man had ever made her want to be completely unrestrained and give everything.

Not until now. What did she have to lose?

After giving Dani another sexy smile, he quickly kissed her, then sat back and started the car. So far, everything was going according to his plan. It did not hurt that she was beautiful, funny, and sexy. All of that was just a bonus. His physical attraction to her was very real.

They drove the next few blocks in silence, each lost in their own thoughts.

Dani watched closely as Sean drove, and turned onto a private road off the main road. Every so often, she glimpsed parts of houses set back from the road deep in the woods surrounding them. At the end of the road, they reached a set of wrought iron gates.

Sean reached forward and pushed a button on the dashboard. The gates opened, revealing a long driveway that led to a red-bricked colonial style house in the distance. As they drew closer, she could just make out the flowers and trees that surrounded the front of the house.

Dani barely felt the car roll to a stop before Sean jumped

out to help her exit. Still holding her hand, he led her towards the front door. She barely had a chance to glance around before Sean pulled her inside.

Sean smiled as he led Dani into the house and directed her through several rooms. He stopped once he reached a set of double doors near the rear of the house.

He slowly opened them and stepped inside. The room flooded with a soft light. The walls of the room were a deep red, serving as the perfect backdrop.

Dani stepped into the room and stared, amazed.

The room contained several statues that looked like originals.

Each statue glowed, displayed perfectly under a soft light. There were seven statues in all. In amazement, Dani stepped forward, realizing that she knew the artists. A stone sculpture by Chidi Okoye fought for attention near a bronze by Leone Leoni.

DANI HAD ALWAYS FELT at home among all forms of Art. She circled each piece, amazed to be so close to such famous pieces. For the first time in her life, she could appreciate the power that came with money. Turning to glance over her shoulder, she saw Sean still standing by the door. For a moment, she had forgotten he was there.

"This is incredible," she said, smiling.

Sean had never let anyone see his private collection. Somehow, with Dani, it seemed right. Rather than buying these pieces because of their value, his home gallery consisted of statues that spoke to him. Like Dani's *The Madonna* had.

Sean shook his head at Dani's comment. "No, you are incredible."

Dani threw Sean an incredulous look. She looked down, blushing. "There's nothing special about me," she said.

Sean's intense stare mirrored his disagreement. The look made Dani nervous. To distract him, she grabbed his hand and led him over to the statues. "Tell me about the statues," she said. "I once had a teacher tell me that there are collectors, and then there are people who buy art because it triggers an emotion deep inside of them." She stopped in front of an Ancient Bronze soldier. "What's the story behind this one?"

Sean regarded the statue through lidded eyes. He remembered vividly buying the soldier. Taking a deep breath, he began speaking.

"This reminded me of my father. When I was younger, he seemed larger than life." Sean reached out and gently brushed his fingers against the bronze face. "He built Davenport Corporation from the ground up, never letting anything or anyone stand in his way. It was nothing for him to work fifty to sixty hour weeks."

The melancholy expression on Sean's face touched Dani's heart as his hand dropped back down to his side. He seemed so lost. "What happened to him?" she asked.

"He died of a heart attack, right before my twenty-fifth birthday." She could feel how close they were through his words.

Dani swallowed the lump that formed in her throat. "I'm sorry."

Sean nodded. "It happened a long time ago."

"And your mother? Is she still alive?"

Sighing, Sean dropped Dani's hand and turned away. "She died seven years ago, the year after my father."

Frowning, Sean quickly left the room. This was not happening as he planned.

CHAPTER 8

*D*ani followed Sean out of the room, taking one last glance behind her. There, in that room, she discovered a piece of the magnanimous Sean Davenport never seen by strangers, and she was humbled. For some reason, though he barely knew her, he opened himself up to Dani, a complete stranger. It made her feel closer to him…very close.

Dani wandered through several rooms before finding Sean in his study.

Strong and pensive, Sean stood behind a desk with his back to the door, holding a glass filled with an amber liquid. He absently tossed back the drink.

"I'm sorry. I didn't mean to pry," Dani said, feeling responsible for Sean's sudden sullen mood. His expression while looking at the statues made him seem so vulnerable. Not at all like the image of the corporate shark she was told he projected to the world. In the room of statues, he seemed so lost.

At least, until he placed his glass on the table and turned

to face her. In those few minutes, as Dani watched Sean's posture and demeanor change, she began to understand.

Sean gave Dani a predatory smile as he turned and sauntered towards her. "You weren't." He felt Dani's body tense as slid his arms around her and eased her against his body. She was so soft and warm. All he could think of was burying himself deep inside her.

Sliding one hand up her back, Sean gently held her in place while leaning down to lightly place a kiss on her neck, lightly nipping the skin as he pulled away. Small tremors ran through Dani's body, her arms lifting up to wrap themselves around Sean.

At that moment, any lingering doubts Dani may have had were gone. Tonight, she would let down her guard and accept everything that Sean would give her. Her body leaned towards Sean as he leaned back. Without a word, he led her from the study. Dani trailed behind him. With no hesitation, Dani followed him down a side hallway and upstairs. He paused in front of a closed set of mahogany doors. Gently cupping her face, Sean lowered his face and captured Dani's lips in a kiss. This kiss was different from the tender nips downstairs. This kiss spoke of hunger and need and... passion. None of them before had made her ache.

Sean stopped the kiss, reached behind him to open the doors, and stepped backwards into a room bathed in soft lights, never once taking his eyes from Dani's. Once inside, he pushed the doors closed, pulling her hard against his body and into a deep kiss before the doors had completely closed.

Dani sighed and strained to move even closer to him, her arms easing up to wrap around his neck in total surrender. Sean's hands moved down Dani's back to cup her ass, drawing her firmly against his growing arousal.

Moving apart, they stared at each other for a moment,

both breathing hard and struggling to come to grips with their unexpected response to each other.

Sean stepped away and led Dani over to the King-sized canopy bed that dominated the room.

"God, I've wanted to do this all night," he muttered hoarsely.

He covered Dani's mouth again before she could speak, peeling her dress down her body little by little, pressing hot kisses across each piece of skin her exposed.

Sean enclosed Dani's silky breast in a single mouth-full. His tongue lapped at the hardened chocolaty nipple. Damn, she tasted like sex. Dani's moans were addictive. He wanted nothing more than to make her scream. Her body clenched as he lightly ran his teeth across the tip. Sean thought he'd lose his mind. He moved to Dani's other breast and feasted there as well, gorging himself as he'd imagined doing since he first set eyes on Dani at the gallery.

Dani threaded her fingers through Sean's hair as her body caught fire. Unconsciously, she ground her legs together, feeling the wetness that gathered between them with every tug of Sean's mouth on her nipples.

Sean raised his head and stripped the dress away from Dani's body. His breath caught in his throat as he realized that she had been without a bra and only wore a skimpy black thong all night. He was rock hard, the front of his pants straining against its expensive fabric. Sean could not remember ever wanting a woman this much. His hands slid down the front of her body to tease the silken curls between her legs before taking her lips again.

Dani pulled away, struggling to catch her breath. "Sean," she panted. "Please!"

Picking her up, Sean laid Dani in the center of the bed. She watched as Sean removed his clothes, tossing them everywhere in his haste. He eased down beside her in the bed. Dani ran her hands over Sean's chest, loving the feel of his skin. In her mind, she pictured his body as a work of art, sleek and strong.

He eased down her body until he was kneeling between her legs. Leaning closer, he inhaled the musky scent of her arousal. Gently he parted the soft curls and sucked gently on the tiny nub nestled within, making her body jerk in response.

Dani moaned as she tried to move away from Sean, her breath coming in short pants as he tortured her with his tongue. He was relentless until he felt her body start to clench. He then carefully inserted first one, then another finger deep inside her.

He almost came when she reached her orgasm, the violence of it leaving her gasping for air, and Sean insane with passion.

Dani's body was like liquid when she felt him start to ease inside her. He pushed forward with short thrusts, savoring the caress of her body surrounding him.

"Look at me baby," he groaned when he reached her barrier.

She opened her eyes, looking up into his eyes as she placed her arms around him, spreading her legs wider. Sean was lost in her gaze, fighting against the feelings she was bringing to life within him. Capturing her lips, he pushed forward into the tightness of her body. A primal sensation surged through his body as he slid deeper. Mine.

Sean felt her stiffen at the pain, but after a few moments, she relaxed and he was able to slide even deeper inside her.

"Damn, you're so tight," he whispered. He pulled almost completely out then pushed back inside her. "Wrap your legs around me."

Dani lifted her legs and wrapped them high around his back. The different angle made him slide deeper inside her.

He stroked back and forth slowly until she managed to catch his rhythm.

"Yes, just like that," Sean groaned. He pushed deeper inside her, making her body arch and tighten around his cock. He could not get enough of her.

"Sean," she groaned. "I – ohh!"

He growled as he felt her body clench around him as he quickened his movements, pushing deeper and harder.

"Damn, Dani!" He panted. He lost control, his body's natural instinct taking control. Over and over again he pushed into her until he erupted inside her, flooding her womb with his seed.

Sean's body twitched as aftershocks pulsed through his body. Since he had always been extremely careful about his partners and himself, he had never known what it felt like to be deep inside of someone without any protection.

He collapsed beside her, pulling her close into the curve of his body.

"Sean, I-,"

"Shh," he said. "Get some rest. I'm by no means through with you." He kissed her forehead and gathered her close while she slept.

Everything was going according to plan.

CHAPTER 9

Still wide awake, Sean waited until Dani slipped into a deep slumber before he eased from the bed. The thick carpet and padding that covered the floor muffled the sound him moving across the floor. With one last glance to ensure she was still sleeping, Sean left the room and went downstairs.

Passing his art room, he traveled further into the house to the room his family used during the rare times his father was home. A portrait of both of his parents, Gregory and Imogene Davenport, seemed to watch him from its position over the fireplace. Sitting on the leather couch that dominated the room, Sean contemplated the life they led. His mother never complained about his father's work hours and to the best of his knowledge, his father never cheated on his mother.

From the stories he heard growing up, Sean's father knew immediately that his mother was the one. Even through his busy schedule, his father, Gregory would stop whatever he was doing to call Imogene – once in the morning, once in the afternoon, and once in the evening. His mother always said that his father's calls demonstrated his feelings more than him being home with her all day.

As much as Sean wanted to experience the white picket fence scenario, his view of marriage was skewed. They did not make women like his mother anymore.

Sean liked Dani, which was a lot more than he expected. She was smart, funny, beautiful and talented. Never once had she made Sean feel like a walking wallet. If anything, she seemed uncomfortable with his wealth.

And wasn't that a novel experience?

"Soon, Dad. I'm not going to let you down." He whispered.

Sean stood and stretched before going back upstairs to sexy woman asleep in his bed.

The soon-to-be mother of his child.

CHAPTER 10

*I*t was still dark outside when Dani felt gentle fingers stroking between her legs. Before she could wake up fully, she was gently rolled on her back while Sean slid deep inside her.

"Good Morning, baby" he whispered in her ear. "How does this feel? Are you too sore? If so, I'll stop."

"No. Hmm. Perfect," she whispered as she opened her legs wide.

"Good." This time Sean moved slowly, keeping his strokes gentle as he eased forward, gritting his teeth at the snug fit of her body wrapped around him, kissing her when he felt her body quicken.

Dani screamed as her body shattered.

Sean moved faster, pulling one of her legs high over his shoulder while stroking deeper and deeper inside her. Dani felt a second orgasm building up inside her.

He wrapped his arms around her as he came, his body shaking from the force of it.

When his heartbeat finally slowed, he kissed her again, tenderly, brushing her hair back from her face.

"You okay?"

She nodded. "Yeah."

"You're not too sore are you?" he asked.

She blushed and looked down. "I didn't think most guys noticed stuff like that."

"I noticed," he said, gently stroking her cheek. "And I'm humbled."

Dani's eyes started to close.

He sat up. "I'll be right back."

She felt him leave the bed, then the sound of water running. She had just begun to doze off when Sean came back and shook her awake. "Come on sleepy head."

He pulled the covers back and lifted her from the bed.

"What are you doing?" Dani asked Sean.

"You're going to be sore," he answered. "You need to soak in a nice hot tub for a little bit."

Carrying Dani into the jade-green Italian-marble master bathroom, he eased her down next to his enormous garden tub. Dani looked around sleepily. "This place is huge." She looked over and saw that the tub was built into the floor. "Nice."

"Come on," he held out his hand so that she could step down into the tub. "Be careful."

He sat down first and pulled Dani back against his chest. "Now, doesn't that feel better?"

"Yes. It's perfect." The scent of lavender rose from the water, relaxing her.

Sean rubbed his hands up and down Dani's body, easing the remaining tension from her muscles. Without realizing it, he found his hands drifting lower on her body until they were stroking the soft curls that covered her mound. Dani's body flared to life again and she wiggled on Sean's lap. Unable to help himself, he eased his fingers inside her, pressing deep inside Dani until her body started to move in time with his hand.

He continued stroking her smoothly with his fingers, while his other hand pinched her nipples. Dani felt Sean's body hardening again behind her and decided two could play that game. She ground against him, smiling to herself when she heard his breath catch.

Sean used his thumb to press against her, making her cry out.

"I can't take anymore!" she moaned, her body shaking wildly.

Turning Dani her around to face him, Sean lifted her up and slid her slowly down his length. "We shouldn't be doing this; you're going to be sore for sure."

"Don't move." Sean laid her against his chest and barely moved inside her. Both of them gently reached their peak together before Dani collapsed against his chest. It was a slow and tender moment between them.

Sean managed to rouse Dani long enough to wash her and lead her back to the bed. She was almost asleep before her head hit the pillow. Sean watched over her until her breathing deepened, then, not questioning what he was doing, he kissed her softly on the forehead.

Sean got up quietly and left the room, walking into his office.

Opening the file on his desk, he calculated forty weeks from the current date. Luckily, he managed to receive the information in time to take advantage of her most fertile cycle. He smiled to himself as he thought of how sexually responsive Dani was to him. It would not hurt for him to continue enjoying her until the pregnancy was confirmed. He was not going to take a chance that anything would happen between now and then.

CHAPTER 11

*D*ani stretched as she woke up later that day and realized instantly that she was not at home. Squinting against the sunlight streaming through the huge windows surrounding her, Dani tried to roll over, only to find herself blocked by a big, hard body snuggled against her.

She froze as the events from last night came back to her. Dani groaned when she realized that she had spent the night with Sean.

"I must have lost my mind," she muttered.

"Not at all." Sean wrapped an arm around Dani to pull her closer to his body.

"Oh, yes. I have."

Sean pulled back slightly, propping himself up on one elbow to look down at Dani. "So I guess that rules out breakfast?"

Turning her head, Dani looked up at him through narrowed eyes. "That depends. Can you cook?"

He smiled, planting a gentle kiss on her shoulder. "I know enough to not burn the toast."

She studied him for a moment. "Okay. I'll stay for breakfast. Then I need to go home."

He eased up off the bed, giving her an excellent view of his butt as he walked across the room. Dani threw the covers back and stood up unsteadily from the bed. He strolled back over a minute later, swinging her dress from his finger.

Sean's eyes smoldered as they roamed over her body. "You might want this. But don't feel forced to wear it on my account."

Dani moved towards Sean, not realizing what a sensual picture she presented walking towards him. Never did he imagine that he would be this attracted to the woman in McKennon's file. She smirked as she took her dress from Sean, slithering into it as he watched.

"Where is my thong?" She asked.

"I couldn't seem to find it," he replied with a straight face. He did not intend to give that particular item of clothing back.

Dani knew he was lying and decided to let it pass.

Knowing that she was too sore to take him again, he crossed his arms to keep from reaching for her and convincing her to go back to bed. For the rest of the day.

Feeling more comfortable now, Dani raised an eyebrow at his lack of clothes. Sighing, he walked into his closet and came back dressed in a pair of sweatpants that had seen better days.

"Better?"

Dani nodded, smiling. "Yes. Less distracting."

Like a predator, Sean's eyes narrowed as they moved over her.

"Hmm? I'm a distraction?" he growled.

"Without clothes?" Dani turned and walked past him. "Oh hell, yes." He caught up to her and grabbed her by the hand, leading her downstairs to his kitchen.

Dani examined everything she had been too distracted to notice the night before. His house was huge, not that she had a comparison. Brand new furniture was scattered around, casually placed in groups. Sean's kitchen contained gleaming stainless steel appliances. One entire wall was nothing but glass with privacy shades pulled low to block out the worst of the midday sunlight.

"Nice place."

"Thanks." Sean looked around as if seeing it for the first time. "I travel a lot, so I don't really get to spend too much time here."

Smiling, Dani took a seat at a glass table near the window. "I can tell. How long have you lived here?"

Sean grabbed a glass from a cabinet, then reached into the refrigerator and removed a carton of orange juice. "You mean according to the tabloids or real time."

He walked over to hand her a glass of orange juice. Dani accepted it and took a small sip, appreciating the feel of the cool liquid sliding down her throat.

"Real time. I don't read tabloids."

Dani watched him move around the kitchen, admiring the way he carefully cracked eggs into the bowl and began to scramble them, then pouring them into the pan.

"I grew up here."

"Never married?" She raised an eyebrow.

Sean watched her cautiously as he answered, "No."

"Kids?"

Sean's lips lifted slightly. "Not yet."

Dani frowned. "What's not yet?" she asked as she watched him place the eggs on two plates.

Sean placed a plate of steaming eggs in front of her before he answered. "Well...I hate to point this out to you, but we made love several times last night, and we didn't use any protection."

Dani's stomach sank. All of a sudden, the perfect omelet sitting in front of her was no longer appealing.

Sean went back for his own plate. "Unless you were taking something?"

She put her face down into her hands. "No. I wasn't. I knew I shouldn't have had that wine last night. What in the hell was I thinking?"

Sean sat down across from her and took her hands in his. "It's okay. I'm as much to blame as you. I swear to you, I've never in my life had unprotected sex with anyone." Dani looked at him skeptically. "Believe me, last night everything just went out of my mind."

He stood and knelt in front of her chair. "It's okay. If we find out you're pregnant, then we'll work through this together." He grasped her chin and pulled her face up to look at him. "I never intended for this to be a one night stand, Dani. I want to keep seeing you, to get to know you better."

Dani shook her head. "Why me? I'm sure you know hundreds of women."

"They only want me because of who I am and what I have." Sean sighed. "Do you know you're the first woman that I've been out with in years who hadn't propositioned me first?"

Against her will, Dani smiled. "After your approach last night? I really find that hard to believe." She shook her head. "I really doubt if we have anything to worry about, but we can take things one step at a time. Okay?"

He nodded. "Fine." Sean walked back to the other side of the table and sat back down. "Good. That's settled. Now eat your eggs." She smiled and picked up a forkful of eggs.

Later on, after they had finished eating, Dani stood staring out of the windows while he got dressed, amazed at the view. Landscaped yard surrounded the house on all sides. If there was a fence in the backyard, it was too far away for

Dani to see. She was so engrossed that she did not hear him come up behind her.

Moving her hair to the side, Sean placed a gentle kiss on the side of her neck. "Are you sure you can't stay a little longer?"

Chills spread through her body at the contact. This man was dangerous to her self-control. "Tempting. Very, very tempting." Dani turned to face him. "But I really need to go."

"All right. If you insist." Sean reluctantly pulled away from her and started towards the door.

Once inside the car, Dani gave him her address then promptly fell asleep. She woke up to a set of lips trailing up the side of her neck. Her eyes snapped open to see Sean inches away from her face while they sat in her driveway.

Dani had been sleeping so peacefully in the passenger's seat that Sean couldn't resist planting a light kiss on her cheek, which led to him sucking on the soft skin at the base of her neck, waking her.

Sighing, Sean sat back in his seat.

Dani looked over at him with a smile. "You are just absolutely devious."

Sean laughed as he left the car to open the door for Dani.

Taking his outstretched hand, she climbed from the car. She was surprised that he held her hand as he walked her to the door.

"So," Sean said when they reached her door, "I'll talk to you later? I already programmed my number into your phone."

With an impish smile, Dani replied, "If I'm awake. I didn't get much sleep last night."

Sean smiled down at her. "Okay. Fair enough," he whispered before capturing her lips.

CHAPTER 12

Dani felt the difference between her house and Sean's when she stepped inside a few minutes later to find the phone ringing off the hook.

"Nobody but Tina," Dani muttered as she picked up the cordless headset.

Tina began yelling before Dani could utter a word. "Dani! Where in the hell have you been? It's two o'clock in the afternoon!"

Dani sighed. "I know Tina…"

"I didn't know if you were alive or dead, whether or not I should call the police…"

"Tina! Breathe!" Dani smiled as she shrugged off her coat and threw it on a nearby chair. Walking into her bedroom, she hit the speakerphone button and placed the phone on the bed while she started to remove her dress. Holding it up, Dani knew she would never look at it the same way again.

Sighing, Dani tossed it on the bed so she could take it to the cleaners later. She pulled an old T-shirt and jeans from her dresser, smiling when she realized that Tina was still fussing. Dani was surprised when Tina stopped her tirade for a minute. "Well? Where were you?"

Dani picked the phone back up drew a deep breath. "I was at Sean's."

"You were with Davenport? All night?"

"Yes, Tina. All night."

The silence on the other end of the line told Dani that Tina's brain was working.

"So…How was he?"

Dani smiled, glad Tina could not see her face. "What do you think?"

"I think," Tina answered, "that if you didn't make it home until two the next afternoon, then he definitely did something right."

"Yeah, there's one small problem though." Dani walked into her bedroom, shuffling the phone from side to side. She was hesitant to mention her problem to Tina. Tina often acted more like her mother than her friend.

It had been that way for most of their life. Tina's family moved in next to Dani's grandfather, where she and her mother lived, when they were in their teens. After Tina's mother died, her father drew into a shell. Dani's mother treated Tina as if she was her own daughter.

They had been inseparable ever since.

"What's that?" Tina asked cautiously.

"It looks like I'm going to have to be on 'watch'" for the next couple of weeks." Dani closed her eyes and waited for the explosion.

"You didn't! I taught you better than that! Come on girl, I know it was your first time, but still! And him! 'Mr. Man of the World!' He definitely knows better!"

Tina went off on a tirade in Spanish that made Dani cringe, even though she didn't know what Tina was saying, just from her tone. Dani heard her puffing as she finally started to calm down.

"Did you even discuss it? You told him that you weren't on anything?"

"Yes. Tina." Dani laid across the bed. "Sean was actually very understanding. He claimed that he hadn't planned for it to be a one night stand anyway and how if I am pregnant, that he's more than willing to accept responsibility for it."

Tina was quiet for a minute. Too quiet. "Hmm."

Dani frowned at the phone. "That's all you have to say is Hmm?"

Tina seemed distracted when she answered. "For now… yeah. So, are you supposed to see him again sometime soon?"

"We hadn't planned on anything. I don't know if I can even face him right now." Dani closed her eyes as she remembered making love with Sean. Her body was already starting to miss his touch.

Tina's sigh brought Dani's attention back to the conversation. "Don't worry about it right now. Chances are with that weird condition you've got that you won't get pregnant anyway."

Dani sat up. "You know something…you're right. I'm probably worrying over nothing. I mean, it's a million to one longshot that he would be the person who could get me pregnant, right?"

"Right. There're women all over the world that wish they had your problem." Tina giggled. "Get some sleep, I'm pretty sure you didn't get much last night."

Dani smiled, feeling better. "Ha ha, funny. I'll call you tomorrow."

"Bye."

Dani hung up the phone and laid back down. Tina was right. She did need to get some sleep.

WHILE DANI SLEPT, Sean paced back and forth in his bedroom on the other side of town trying to decide his next course of action. He had surprised himself with his reluctance to take Dani home, but he had not wanted to move too fast. Sean's whole body ached for Dani again as he thought about last night, the way her body responded to his. He rubbed his hands over his face. A cold shower was just the thing to take his mind off her and help him get some sleep.

CHAPTER 13

A gnawing ache for food pulled Dani from a deep slumber the next morning, where a black-haired, green-eyed phantom wreaked havoc on her body. She rose from her bed and stumbled to the shower. Afterwards, she dried off quickly, dressed, got her morning cup of coffee and toast. Taking a deep sigh, she headed for her studio.

Dani toyed with a new block of marble Clayton found for her, but she had no idea what to create. All she could see was Sean's face. It felt like she stared at it for hours before something came to mind. She walked over to her little beat up radio and turned it on. Grabbing her chisel and hammer, she began to go to work letting the soothing rhythm of the music wash over her.

Sean pulled up to Dani's house and parked behind her car. Walking to the front door, he rang the doorbell and turned around to look at his surroundings. Nice neighborhood. Sean waited a few moments, but there was no answer. Thinking Dani might be in the shower, he rang the bell again several times, still not receiving an answer.

Starting to become concerned, Sean walked around to

Dani's garage. He breathed a sigh of relief when he heard the steady sound of a hammer tapping. He headed for the door, stopped at its side and turned the knob, surprised to find it unlocked.

He stepped in quietly, not wanting to disturb Dani at work. Her sleeveless t-shirt and shorts were covered in dust. Music played blasted in the background, which would explain why she did not hear the doorbell. Sean watched in amazement as Dani brought depth and texture to a slab of marble.

She was amazing.

Sean eased slowly over into Dani's line of vision. The last thing he wanted was to startle her. Her eyes widened when she saw Sean standing in front of her. She walked over to the radio and turned it down.

"Hi," Dani said, surprised. "I didn't expect to see you today."

Sean shrugged. "I know. I was hoping maybe I could take you out for lunch."

Dani frowned. "Lunch?"

A chill went through Sean's body as Dani rubbed her stomach. "I didn't realize it was so late. I forgot to eat breakfast. I only had a piece of toast."

One of Sean's eyebrows rose. "Then its good I showed up when I did."

Dani watched Sean closely as he walked over to her. He looked delicious. Unruly black locks dipped down over his forehead, nearly meeting the long black lashes that framed his eyes. He wore a black long sleeved shirt that hung loose outside of a form a dark pair of jeans that gave a teasing outline of the muscles beneath. She loved him in casual clothes.

Her skin tingled as he cupped her face in his hands.

"It looks like you need someone to look after you." Sean

touched his lips to Dani's, deepening the pressure until she responded. He pulled back slowly.

"Why don't you go take a quick shower and we'll go get something?"

She stared at him for a moment. "What are you up to?" Dani whispered.

Startled, Sean let his hands drop from her face. "I'm not up to anything," he said, his tone becoming cold. "I'm just trying to spend some time with you."

Sean's reaction made Dani feel low. Evidently, she had been cooped up in the studio too long if she had to be suspicious of everything he said. She sighed. "I'm sorry. Maybe I am reading too much into this." She nodded. "Okay. If I haven't pissed you completely off and the offer still stands, I'd love to have lunch with you."

Butterflies churned in Dani's stomach when Sean smiled. Before she could have second thoughts, he turned her around and pushed her towards the door.

CHAPTER 14

While Sean waited for Dani to shower and dress in the house, he walked around her makeshift studio, mentally making a list of all the materials and equipment she had. During the last months of her pregnancy, Sean wanted to be able to duplicate her studio, to make sure he could keep her close by. Things that looked strange to him, he took pictures of with his phone. He would get someone to identify the items later.

By the time Dani returned to the studio, dressed in a pair of jeans and a V-neck sweater that hugged and caressed her curves, Sean had managed to catalog everything inside. Dani had pulled her hair up into a ponytail, making her look years younger. The hairdo made Sean realize what Dani had looked like as a child. Or what their child would look like.

Sean locked eyes with Dani and felt that nothing else mattered at this moment. No woman had ever made him want to take time away from work – his legacy – just to spend time with them. He broke eye contact to take one last long, heated gaze at Dani's body.

He held out his hand to her.

Stepping forward, Dani placed her hand in his. The slightest touch from Sean warmed her body. Dani got the strange sensation that nothing was going to be the same after today.

Sean took her to a different restaurant this time, a small, quiet place near the water called Baywatch. From their booth, they watched the boats sailing in the distance.

"This is so peaceful," Dani said, turning to Sean. She studied his profile while he gazed out of the window. She was still in disbelief that this man was interested in her.

"Good," Sean said taking her hands. "I wanted someplace quiet and peaceful where we could get to know each other."

Dani smirked. "Do you by chance own this one, too?"

"No." Sean looked around. "As a matter of fact, I haven't been here in quite a while." Kissing the palm of her hand, Sean smiled at her. "Tell me about you."

Dani told Sean how she discovered the art of carving from her grandfather at the age of six. "He made the funniest little characters for me. I always loved it when he made them. But I never liked how the wood would split and crack. When I was in Junior High, I had a chance to go to an art gallery that dealt primarily in sculptures." Dani shrugged. "That was it. I found my calling. I worked on them for several years, and then..." She took a sip of her water. "Then mother and grandfather died within a few months of each other." Dani took a deep breath to pull herself together. "I stopped for a while. I couldn't seem to... to find the will to work anymore. With them gone, it seemed like it was all for nothing."

Pasting on a smile, she asked Sean, "What about you?"

"There's not much to tell." Sean shrugged, pulling his hands away from hers. Dani could almost feel the barriers drop into place around him. "I was an only child. My father started Davenport Corporation before I was born. Everything I learned, every school I went to, it was understood that it was all in preparation for me to take over the company."

Dani studied his face closely, searching for some sign of emotion. There was none.

"I'm going to guess…that you guys weren't very close."

Sean looked up into her eyes expecting to see sarcasm, but instead found himself touched at the compassion that shimmered there. "No. We weren't. Not really."

Dani reached back across the table for Sean's hand and linked her fingers through his.

Sean looked at their hands laced together, his paler skin linked with her dark, smooth fingers, then back into Dani's eyes. She understood what he felt. The loneliness and the pain inside that kept him emotionally apart from everyone, preventing him from having a solid relationship. Dani was refreshing and honest…and soon to be the mother of his child.

Sean leaned across the table to kiss Dani then froze when a willowy beauty walked up, straight from the pages of Vogue.

Dani looked up, puzzled, expecting to see the server returning to take their order.

Sean's face drained of emotion as he eyed the gorgeous brunette in a form-fitting couture dress slinking up to his table.

The turquoise shade of the woman's outfit perfectly matched the color of her eyes. Her pale skin was enhanced by her perfect makeup. Her hair flowed around her shoulders, not a split end in sight. Dani was glad that she had gotten her hair done before the show so that she wouldn't feel so frumpy in this chick's presence.

She hated the woman on sight.

"Sean!" the brunette squealed. Dani tried to pull her hand

back from Sean's only to find that he wouldn't let go. She ignored Dani completely.

"I've missed you the past few weeks. Where have you been?"

Dani's hackles rose. She understood that she was not in the supermodel category, but there was no way she was going to let this woman ignore her when she was sitting right in plain sight. The spark of jealously Dani felt did not help the situation. She could tell that this woman travelled in the same circles as Sean. Rich and privileged.

She was probably a Republican.

Sean cursed under his breath as he recognized the woman. Sabrina Terry. The last thing he needed was her popping up, ruining his plans. "Sabrina, I thought I made it clear that I didn't want to see you again." The tone of his voice let everyone within hearing distance know that he was not happy to see the woman.

Dani's was about to speak, when her mouth snapped closed. Gone was the easy-going man that had been sitting across from her. If he used this trick in the boardroom, it was no wonder he was able to takeover companies with virtually no problems.

The woman – Sabrina – tried to laugh it off. "I didn't pay you any mind, silly." She tossed her hair back over her shoulder. "I knew you were just upset because of all the attention I got at the Werner's party. I figured you just needed some time to calm down."

"Sabrina, I don't give a damn who you flaunt yourself in front of. I told you from the beginning not to expect anything from me. You deluded yourself. Now if you'll excuse me, my date and I would like to eat in peace."

Dani watched in amazement as Sabrina turned beet red to bright pink, and finally pale dead white. Sabrina turned on her heels, left the table, and returned to the other side of the room. However, not before turning to Dani with a look so hateful, Dani almost forgot to breathe.

Sean squeezed Dani's hands. "I'm sorry about that. Would you like to go somewhere else?"

Dani took a deep breath. "No. I'm fine. What did you do to that woman? Long stroke when you should have been short stroking?"

Sean surprised himself when laughter burst out of him, his first genuine laughter in months. He was always so serious, concentrating on business matters, that he couldn't remember the last time he actually enjoyed himself.

"No," he said when he could finally catch his breath. "Sabrina loved my bank account."

Sean smiled wider when Dani muttered under her breath, "I'll bet there's a lot there to love." He laughed again. Holding tight when she would have pulled away, Sean would not let her hands go until their food arrived. They ate in silence, occasionally sneaking glances at each other. When she was not looking at Sean, Dani kept one eye on her food and one eye on the woman who had stopped by the table. Every so often Sabrina would look over at Dani as if she wanted to pick up her salad fork and jab it into Dani's eyes.

Dani was glad when they finally left, but she did not believe for a moment that Miss Brunette was going to give up that easily.

CHAPTER 15

*N*ight was falling when they arrived back at Dani's house. To her surprise, most of the day was gone. If Sean had not shown up, her day would have been consumed by her sculpting. She could not remember the last time she spent a day away from her work.

Sean pulled into the driveway and placed the car in park. Before Dani could tell him that she had had a nice time and try to get away, Sean had gotten out and was opening her door. Dani was nervous as she walked towards the front entrance with Sean close behind her. She turned and considered trying to send Sean away, but reconsidered. Sean was watching her with that intense gaze again. Without saying anything, Dani opened the door and let Sean follow her inside.

His eyes narrowed as she walked through the door, kicked off her shoes and stretched out on the couch. He found that sexy as hell. Dani turned him on just lying there.

"Oh god, I'm so full I can't move." Dani groaned, stretching and throwing her arms above her head, causing her breasts to push up against her top.

Sean tossed his jacket onto a nearby chair and walked over to the couch. He liked the look of her house. It was comfortable. Family pictures and knick-knacks hung lovingly around the living room. The furniture, like the couch Dani stretched across, was made to be used by families, not to be used as a decoration. It was more than a house; it was a home.

Dani squinted up when she sensed Sean standing over her.

"What do I get if I can make you move?" Sean asked, huskily. Lifting her, he pulled her onto his lap, wrapping his arms around Dani to hold her close against the solid wall of his chest.

She relaxed against him until she felt him harden beneath her. "Umm, I'm awake now." Pushing her hands between them, she stroked along the rising bulge in his pants. "Looks like someone else is awake, too," she murmured. Dani smiled, feeling powerful, knowing that she was able to garner this response in him.

"Oh yes, wide awake," Sean replied as he worked his hands under Dani's top and unfastened her bra. Sean pushed his hips against Dani as his hands worked magic on her breasts, plucking and pulling at her nipples. One hand left her breasts to rub along her body, spreading heat everywhere they touched.

Dani's body jerked as Sean reached between her legs and pressed against the seam of her jeans. His fingers circled around the area, not touching her there again, making her squirm.

"Baby, where's your room?" he whispered, kissing her gently on her neck.

"Oh… in the back." Sean helped Dani up off of his lap, then stood and led her towards the bedroom, stopping every few steps to kiss her and pull clothes from her body. Once

Sean had Dani naked, he picked her up and dropped her in the middle of the bed. He quickly undressed and laid beside her, his hands roaming over her body. He could not stop touching her.

"Can I stay tonight?" Sean asked before leaning over to capture a nipple in his mouth. Dani squirmed as he ran his teeth across it.

"All night?" Dani whispered. If he kept that up, he could stay forever.

"Umm hmm." Sean moved to her other breast and feasted.

"Oh yes." Dani whimpered. "Definitely, absolute-," she gasped as his mouth moved down her body, his tongue tracing circles across her skin until he reached her soaking wet center. Dani's body jerked as his fingers parted her curls and tenderly touched the tiny nub. With a devilish smile, Sean leaned forward and began sucking gently on her, easing two fingers deep inside her, slowly stroking them in and out of her body. Dani's moved in time with him until her body exploded, leaving her shaking and breathless.

"Sean," she panted, grabbing his hair. "I need you."

Sean groaned, lifting Dani's legs over his shoulders and pushed to the hilt inside her, the movement sending her over the edge once again. He fought to stay still inside her, not ready to have it over so soon. His body shook with the effort of holding back. Once Dani's breathing returned to normal, Sean let her legs fall, and then wrapped his arms around her. He set a slow, steady pace, stroking back and forth.

Sean watched Dani's face as she began responding to him once again. Lowering his head, he began kissing her. He sucked gently just above her collarbone, leaving a noticeable love bite. His mark. The sight of it roused something primitive inside of him. Sean wanted to mark Dani on the inside, too. He wanted to ruin her for any other man.

He heard someone groaning and realized that it was him.

Sean heard Dani whimpering his name as her body began to pulse tightly around him, pulling the seed from his body. Sean stayed up on his elbows, not wanting to put his full weight on Dani. He rolled to his side, pulling her with him, holding her tight in his arms.

Dani fought a losing battle to keep her eyes open. She was satisfied but drained. All she could do was enjoy the feeling of being safe and protected in Sean's arms. Just before she fell asleep, she heard Sean whisper in her ear. "Does that count as a long stoke?"

She smiled sleepily. "Oh, yes. Absolutely."

"Good," Dani thought she heard Sean mutter as she fell asleep.

CHAPTER 16

Sean woke Dani up early the next morning before he left. She savored the feeling of him spooning her from behind. "I've got to go to work baby." Dani groaned while he smiled down at her.

He dropped a kiss down on the soft brown skin of her shoulder, smiling as he watched her cover her head. Sean pulled her closer.

Dani could barely open her eyes.

"Why don't you give me something to think about while I'm there?" Sean lifted Dani's leg and slid inside her from behind. Her body immediately came to life beneath his hands. He could easily fall in love with this woman.

Sean closed his eyes and enjoyed the sensation of being inside Dani. Until now, he had never wanted someone all the time. One look at Dani and he wanted nothing more than to stay in bed with her all day. This time there was no urgency, just a sweet and tender moment between them.

Dani grumbled slightly as she felt Sean lift her from the bed.

"Take a shower with me, sleepyhead." Dani smiled as she thought of the difference between Sean's bathroom and hers.

Holding her hands, Sean helped Dani walk into the bathroom. He turned on the shower and then adjusted the temperature. After a few moments under the shower's spray, Dani opened her eyes.

"I can see you and I aren't going to get along," she mumbled.

Sean laughed at her pouting while he began to soap her body. "And why is that?"

Dani sighed in contentment as Sean ran soapy hands over her breasts. "You're too damn chipper in the morning."

Sean laughed as he leaned in to kiss her.

Dani was growing on him.

ani went back to sleep the minute Sean left. He had managed to attack her again in the shower. Where in the hell did he get the energy? He was going to make some woman a hell of a husband someday.

After waking up around midday, Dani grabbed something light to eat and went into the studio. She managed to work the whole day undisturbed, mainly because she had left her cordless phone in the house.

Dani almost jumped out of her skin when she looked up to find Tina standing in front of her, arms folded, tapping her foot. "I don't know why I have to come down here and act like your mama."

Dani smiled. "Whassup, girl?"

"That's what I want to know." Tina stepped forward through the dust. "God, don't you ever clean this place up?"

"I'm used to it."

Tina brushed off the loveseat and sat down. Dani had to admire her friend's outfit. Tina wore three-inch high fuchsia heels, with a form fitting dark blue sheath. All her accessories managed to coordinate with her shoes, including the mini pouch that was not big enough to hold Dani's car keys.

"I tried to call you yesterday and this morning," Tina said arching an eyebrow.

Dani blushed. "Sean came by and took me to lunch yesterday afternoon."

"A Sunday brunch, hmm. And then?"

"And then what?" Dani did not volunteer anything else, just brushed dust from her statue.

Dani focused on the statue, but a quick glance confirmed that Tina's eyes narrowed. Only Tina could make her feel like a five year-old, even though she was two years older. "You slept with him again didn't you?"

She sighed as she placed the brush down on the table. "Yes, Tina."

"Dani, I know the sex is probably good…," she stopped at the expression on Dani's face and decided to try a different approach.

"Okay, it's damn good. I just don't want you to get hurt. This guy is known for changing women more often than some people change their drawers. I mean, I know I encouraged you to do it, but let's be honest. According to the papers, he's been avoiding marriage for years."

"I know, Tina. It's okay. I'm not looking for a husband. Especially not a million dollar playboy husband. When I'm ready for a husband, it'll be for love. Somebody who I feel like I can trust not to have women running after him every moment of the day."

Tina raised an eyebrow. "So you're going to marry an ugly man?"

Dani laughed. "Haven't you heard? Women are after the ugly ones, too."

"Right, you're right." Tina looked at her watch. "Just be careful. He's up to something. I just came by to tell you that you have to get down to the studio before Clay loses his mind. Oh, and you'll be proud to know that I did behave myself the other night."

"Good Girl." Dani nodded. "I don't think Clay can deal with any more irate wives."

Tina smiled. "Me either."

CHAPTER 18

Sean stared out of the huge windows of his office, thinking back to earlier that morning. Over the past month, he and Dani had fallen into a pattern. She worked on her sculptures during the day, and he went to work. They spent their evenings quietly at Dani's house or at a restaurant before going back to Sean's house.

Last night, he stayed at Dani's house. He brought Chinese food with him so she could finish some minor work on her latest statue. It all felt so domestic.

Leaving her this morning was one of the hardest things Sean ever did. His entire focus was beginning to shift, and he needed to bring things back on track.

He picked up the phone and dialed Dani's number. Sean frowned when she did not answer, but figured she was in her shop working.

"Hi Dani, it's Sean. I have to take care of some business out of town. I'm going to be in Italy for the rest of the week. I'll call you when I get back."

He hung up the phone slowly, and then buzzed his assistant.

"I need my plane readied for a flight to Italy. I need to be in the air no later than three o'clock."

"Yes, Mr. Davenport."

Sean looked at his watch. One-thirty. Just enough time to get home and pack up what he would need for the next week. Standing up, he had just begun to pack up his papers when his assistant buzzed him.

"McKennon's here Mr. Davenport."

"Send him in."

He watched as his head of security, and long-time friend walked in the door. For some reason, McKennon always reminded him of the man who used to play the cowboy detective in that old TV show, McCloud. His father always liked to watch it on the rare times he was at home. McKennon's slow drawl gave people the idea that he was a slow hick, but the man had one of the sharpest minds Sean had ever come across.

"Leaving already Davenport?" McKennon said, smiling.

Sean smiled. "I need to close out this deal in Italy. I'll be gone about a week."

McKennon nodded. "Just figured I'd check with you about the other situation since I hadn't heard back from you."

"Actually, I've already put something in motion," Sean said cautiously.

"Oh? So you did approach her about it? Did she agree?"

Sean stopped packing up his briefcase and placed his hands on his hips. "I didn't…exactly make her an offer. After I read her file, I came to the same conclusion you did."

"That she wouldn't agree?" McKennon shrugged. "So what are you going to do?"

"I had to move on to plan B."

McKennon crossed his arms and stared at Sean before responding. "Sean, I've known you for many years, but I have to honestly say that even though I don't have a clue as to what you're doing, I'm pretty sure I'm not going to like it."

Sean had known McKennon for over twenty years, learning from him the little nuances his father did not have a chance to teach him before he died. "And I get the feeling you're not going let this rest," Sean continued.

"Nope," McKennon said, getting comfortable in a nearby chair.

Sean sighed and sat back down in his chair. Keeping himself as detached as possible, he donned his persona as the calculating CEO and outlined his complete plan to McKennon. The further he got into his plan, the more McKennon's face registered complete disbelief.

"Sean, you can't be serious!" McKennon walked over and leaned forward on the desk. "Do you think she'll give the child up to you without a fight? For god's sake, Sean! With the exception of her two friends, she's alone in the world! Her father died when she was a baby and her mother and grandfather passed on just a few years ago. The only family she'd have in this world would be that child."

"You just don't get it, do you?" McKennon shook his head. "There's going to be a bond there between her and that child. A deep, strong bond. This isn't one of those little money grubbing debutantes you like to screw around with."

Sean sighed, rubbing his hands over his face, his expression weary. "I know that, McKennon."

"So you need to tell her what's going on."

Sean shook his head. "I can't," he sighed. "It's too late. She will hate me, and I'll never get to see the child. The only thing to do now is follow it through."

"Is it really all about the child? And how do you know she's even pregnant?"

"I just know. That first night-," Sean broke off, shaking his head.

McKennon searched Sean's eyes closely. "You're still sleeping with her aren't you?"

He avoided McKennon's gaze and reached down to close his briefcase. "Just to be on the safe side."

"Yeah…I'll bet." To Sean's surprise, McKennon smiled and turned to walk out of the door. "Just be careful that you don't get caught up in your own lies." The gruff detective stepped out and softly closing the door behind him.

Sean watched McKennon leave and sat back down in his chair. McKennon was right. Sean was in deeper than he wanted to admit. He just hoped it did not blow up in his face.

Ms. Davis buzzed him shortly after pulling him out of his daydream.

"Yes, Ms. Davis."

"Mr. Davenport, your pilot said he'll be ready to lift off by 2:30."

"Thank you, Ms. Davis."

Sean forced himself out of the chair and towards the door.

CHAPTER 19

*D*ani came out of the garage and saw the light blinking on her answering machine. She frowned as she heard Sean's message, then the one from Tina. Grabbing her cordless, she took it with her into the kitchen as she quickly threw together a sandwich. She dialed Tina's number.

"Hey, chica!" Tina answered.

Dani laughed. She loved it when Tina was upbeat. "Hey, Tina. What's up?"

"That depends. Are you hanging with your boy Sean tonight?"

Dani pouted. "No. He left me a message saying he's going to be in Italy for the rest of this week."

"Um, hm, probably going to see some skinny plastic skank with silicone boobs."

Dani could not help her burst of laughter. "Thanks a lot, Tina!"

"What you need is a night out. You never go anywhere, and Lord knows it's gotten even worse since you've been with lover boy. I don't have a problem with people getting their freak on, but you two need to come up for air sometime!"

"That's not all we do, you know," Dani sputtered.

"Sure it's not. You're in denial, all the more reason for you to go out tonight. Besides, it will be good for him to see you don't have to sit home and wait for him to show up. Be dressed when I get there at six. Don't make me come looking for you!" Tina said.

Laughing, Dani had to take a deep breath before she could answer. "Okay, girl. Okay!"

Hanging up the phone, Dani padded into the bedroom to look at her closet's meager offerings. The only thing that looked remotely appropriate was the dress she wore to the gallery for her showing – that she had just picked up from the cleaners. "Oh well. I might as well get some more wear out of it."

Dani showered, curled her hair, and was ready within minutes of Tina pulling up to her door.

Nodding her approval, Tina grabbed Dani's arm and pulled her out the door. "Perfect. Let's go!"

Tina dragged Dani to her favorite club, Dynasty. Latin beats pumped around her as they walked in and found a table. Dani still was not sure what the thrill was about club hopping. Every club Dani had ever been in was the same. A bunch of guys standing on the wall, scoping you out as you walk in, trying to feed you drinks so they can get laid. Tina was definitely a regular. Dani watched as person after person came to their table, some of them to talk to Tina, others trying their luck at making Dani the next notch on their belt. Dani danced with a couple of guys who seemed interesting, but they had so many hands it felt like dancing with an octopus. It was not until around 3 a.m. that she thought to look in her purse for her cellphone.

"Damn!"

Tina looked over and at her and frowned. "What's the matter?"

"No! I left my cellphone at home!"

A conniving smile appeared on Tina's face. "You didn't leave it. I took it out of your purse. Who were you really going to talk to on that little pay-as-you-go number?" Tina gave Dani a dismissive wave. "You only buy ten minutes at a time anyway. The last thing you need to do is use them trying to call Davenport. If he wants you to call him, tell him to put you on his plan." Tina tossed back her drink and began to wiggle in her seat to the music. "The purpose of you coming out with me was so that he won't think you have no life…well, you don't… but he doesn't have to know that."

Chuckling, Dani took a sip of her drink. Tina was right. Although they had spent a lot of time together over the past week, neither had officially made a commitment to the other. Regardless of how she felt about Sean, he was free to see other people and so was she. So, when the next person asked her to dance, she accepted.

For the most part, Dani had fun. Her feet hurt from dancing and she was a little tipsy from the wine she drank. Dani noticed that Tina kept her drinks to a minimum, probably because she was driving.

Sometime around 6 a.m., Dani let herself into the house and quickly undressed as she walked into her bedroom. She was too tired to bother looking for one of her nightshirts and crawled between the sheets in just her panties. The sheets were chilly.

After sleeping beside Sean for the past month, it felt strange to be alone in bed. She drifted off to sleep thinking of a pair of sexy green eyes. A loud ringing noise in Dani's ear woke her several hours later.

It rang several times before she realized it was the telephone.

"Hello?"

"Hey, baby." Sean's deep, smooth voice soothed Dani, bringing a smile to her face. "I've been trying to reach you."

"Hey, yourself." Dani stretched, smiling.

"Were you asleep? I'm sorry. I just got in from a meeting. I just knew I wanted to talk to you. I tried calling your cell a couple of times and figured you were in your studio. I'm sorry I woke you."

"It's okay. Tina wanted to go clubbing. I didn't get home until 6."

"Oh," Sean was quiet for a moment. The thought of her hanging out in the club with all those single men did not sit well with Sean. "Did you have fun? I'm sure every man there wanted to dance with you."

Dani shrugged, forgetting that Sean could not see her through the phone. "It was okay. The guys all seem to have a million hands. All the men love Tina, really. But there were a few that approached me." She smiled. "I wore the dress I was wearing the night we met."

Sean saw red. It took all of his willpower not to comment. He did not want anyone else to see Dani in that dress. He hesitated before continuing.

"Did you meet anyone…interesting?" Sean wanted to kick himself for asking the question, but he needed to know.

"Ugh. At a club? No way! They're all hounds." Dani yawned, her body telling her that she needed to go back to sleep. "I miss you."

Dani's words put Sean's mind at ease. "I miss you, too. Go get some sleep. I'm going to try to finish everything up as soon as possible to get back. Okay?"

Dani's eyes were closing, though she longed to continue talking to Sean. "Okay. I'll see you then."

"Bye." Sean hung up the phone and lay back on the bed. What made him call? True, he wanted to check on her, but it would not be wise to become too attached to Dani. He kept telling himself that he had to stay focused on his goal, but he could not pull himself away.

Later on that evening, Sean laid in his bed alone, tossing and turning. As he stared at the ceiling, he realized he needed to face the facts. He was thousands of miles away from home, surrounded by beautiful, voluptuous Italian women.

And all he wanted was Dani.

CHAPTER 20

*D*ani awoke later that evening, half her body hanging off the bed, with a pounding headache. Gingerly, she made her way into the bathroom, opening her eyes just enough to find the aspirin. She quickly downed two, returned to her bed, discarded her clothes, and eased gently between the covers.

She slept through the rest of the night, managing to feel well enough that night to get something to eat the next morning. Dani thought about the call from Sean, which was definitely unexpected. Sean just came in out of nowhere and swept her off her feet. The more time she spent with him, the more she wanted to be with him. Until he called from Italy, she had begun to wonder if Sean viewed their relationship as strictly sexual.

Dani started towards her workshop, but changed her mind and went back to bed. Today was going to be a lazy day. Maybe she would even catch up on some shows she missed.

She was surprised when her phone rang shortly after she

laid back down. Hoping it was Sean, she smiled and rolled over to answer it.

"Hello?"

"Dani?"

Cringing, she shifted the phone to the other ear and tried to think of something to say.

"*Damn*," she thought. It was Clay.

She had been so wrapped up in Sean that she had completely forgotten about Clay. She was never going to hear the end of it.

"Hi, Clay. Sorry I haven't called you. You know how I am when I get wrapped up in my work." Dani cringed, hoping he would accept the excuse.

"Um hm. I bet. You've been all caught up with the playboy."

Dani crossed her fingers, hoping she would not go to hell for the lie she was about to tell. "Nooooo...actually I've been working."

"Well, that's good news at least. Did Tina tell you I said to come past the studio?"

"Yeah, she did. I actually planned on coming by today."

"Good. We definitely need to talk. You, my dear, got a call here about a commission."

Dani almost dropped the phone in shock. "You're kidding, right? Where?"

"Some hotel they're building on the West Coast. Somewhere in Seattle. They want a ten-foot statue for their front foyer, something original. There's only one catch."

Dani frowned. "What's that?"

Clayton paused before speaking. "They need it in three months."

For a moment, all Dani could do was stand there in disbelief. "Clay, that's a hell of a time crunch for a ten foot statue."

Clayton sighed. "I know, but they're willing to offer you a one hundred and twenty five thousand dollar commission."

Dani gasped. No one had ever offered her that much for her work before.

"Minus my ten percent commission, of course," Clayton added.

Laughter bubbled up inside Dani. "Of course. I guess I'd better start some drawings for them."

"Perfect. I'm going to rent a space for you to work in. Lord knows you can't work in that little garage. Oh, and they want us to fly out on Friday, so that you can look at the hotel and get a feel for the place."

"The day after tomorrow?"

"Yeah. So that you can get started as soon as possible."

Dani looked at the calendar. That meant if she did not see Sean before she left, then it would probably be a few days before she talked to him again.

"Okay, just call me back with the flight times. I'm going to go start packing and do some preliminary sketches."

"I'll call you in the morning." Clay hung up without saying goodbye. Typical Clayton.

Dani hung up the phone in a daze and walked towards her bedroom. She started to call Tina but hesitated. The person Dani really wanted to share her good news with was Sean.

After hunting around the house for ten minutes, she found her cell phone and saw where Sean had called her, several times. She paused for a moment before calling him back, unsure of how Sean would react. Deciding that she was being silly, Dani punched his name on the list and waited for it to ring.

"Davenport."

"Hi, Sean."

"Dani? Is everything okay?" Sean sounded worried.

"No, everything's, fine." Dani laughed. "It's better than fine. I've been commissioned to do a statue for a hotel on the West Coast."

"Really? That's great. I'm so proud of you. It's good that other people have finally started to recognize your talent. You'll be famous in no time."

Dani felt truly validated. The rich and powerful Sean Davenport had given her his blessing. "I don't know about the famous part," she said blushing. "But taking the job means I'm not going to be here for a few days. They want me to go look at the hotel and submit some sketches."

Sean was quiet for a moment before he responded. "Which hotel?"

Dani frowned. "I forgot to ask. It's somewhere in Seattle. All I know is that they've just finished building it. Clay has all the details. I just told him to call me with the flight info."

Sean laughed. "Aren't you a little concerned that he could be sending you out into the middle of nowhere?"

"Clayton? No. Not really. We've been friends a long time. Besides…Clay wants his ten percent commission."

The deep, the husky sounds of Sean's voice shot through her, making her wish that he was there with her, his body pressed against hers.

"Dani?"

Dani blushed again as she realized Sean must have been talking to her while she fantasied about his body. "Yeah, I'm here. I, um, just wanted to let you know what my schedule will look like for the near future."

"Let me know when you get back, okay?"

"Okay. Talk to you later."

"Bye."

"Bye."

Dani hung up the phone and sighed. She was in way too deep.

CHAPTER 21

Sean hung up the phone and rolled over. It was no use trying to deny what was happening. Closing his eyes, he pictured Dani as he had last seen her; her head thrown back in ecstasy, hair spread across the pillow, her body wrapped around his. He had pushed deeper and deeper inside her. The memory of the force of his release had him hard and aching for her.

He wondered if she was pregnant yet and shocked himself at the feelings it aroused. Not just at the thought of having a child, but the vision of Dani round and carrying his child. Sean rubbed his hands over his face and pulled himself together. Tossing back the covers, he headed for the shower to prepare for his day.

CHAPTER 22

Sean hated that he did not make it home from Italy until Dani had already left. He thought about surprising her and making a trip to the hotel. He had McKennon check hotels in Seattle that had just completed construction to determine where she was staying. The hotel, Excalibur, was expected to become one of the premier hotels on the West Coast.

Being able to have one of her statues on display would be huge for Dani. Sean had almost called and booked the trip until he realized that showing up unexpected could be disruptive to her work. Dani never interfered with his work. She was never clingy or needy. Her self-sufficiency was evident in everything she did.

Instead, Sean went home miserable and worked. Most days, he was in the office by 7 a.m. and worked until 9 or 10 at night. Even though he was working his usual long hours, Sean's staff noticed a change in him.

McKennon was the one who finally approached him about it.

Sean was working late one night when McKennon strolled into his office without knocking.

"You do know the staff is talking about you."

Looking up from the papers scattered all over his desk, Sean frowned. "Talking about me?"

Nodding, McKennon took a seat on a nearby couch. "They've noticed that you're withdrawn. Mind you, they already considered you standoffish, I don't know why, considering what a nice, friendly boss you've always been."

Pinching the bridge of his nose, Sean attempted to stave off the headache he felt building.

"I'm too tired for your sarcasm this evening," Sean muttered. "Don't you have some hacker you need to track down?"

McKennon made himself comfortable and crossed one leg over another, flashing a pair of black and red hand stitched cowboy boots that had seen better days.

"Nope. You hired them all to find your perfect woman. The woman who, I'm guessing, is the cause of your current dilemma."

Sean dropped his hand to the desk and sat back. "And what dilemma would that be?"

"The dilemma of you being on the East coast, and Ms. Knox being on the West Coast."

"How did you know she was on the West Coast?"

Tilting his head, McKennon just stared at Sean.

"Of course you would know," Sean muttered. "We're not married. She's a grown woman. She can go wherever and do whatever she wants."

Smirking, McKennon sat up. "Stop the macho crap, Sean. You care about the girl. Admit that it's killing you that she's not here."

Sean opened his mouth several times to deny it, but nothing came out. He sighed. "I miss her. I figured if I worked until I was exhausted, I wouldn't miss her as much. She's only been gone a few days, but it seems longer." Sean shook his head. "I've gotten so used to sleeping with her at her house, I can't sleep in my bed without her."

A bright smile stretched across McKennon's face. "You poor sap. You've got it bad." McKennon stood and stretched his legs. "Staying here and working yourself to death isn't going to solve the problem. I have it on good authority that she's flying in tomorrow. The last thing you want is to look like shit when she gets back."

Laughing, Sean stood and grabbed his jacket from the back of his chair. "I really hate it when you're right. So, what do I owe you for your counseling session today?"

"A couple of glasses of that hundred-year-old scotch you've got stashed at your place is sufficient payment."

Sean nodded and laughed as he followed McKennon out of the office.

CHAPTER 23

A jubilant Clayton and an exhausted Dani found themselves in the back seat of a taxi coming back from the West Coast after nearly a week. Passing the familiar landmarks, Dani realized that no matter where she went, she would always be happiest when she came home.

Glancing over, Dani watched Clayton fidget next to her in his seat. Dani could understand why he was excited. This would be the largest commission Clayton had ever handled. Dani smiled as she looked over at him, still dressed head to toe in black. Clayton always had an eye for the dramatic.

Dani had always been comfortable around Clayton, maybe because she knew he wasn't going to make any demands on her. When her mother and grandfather died, he had been her shoulder to lean on.

It had been Clayton and Tina's shoulders Dani had cried on when she received the news about her blood disorder and the possibility that she would never have children. In many ways, she felt that Clayton deserved the credit for her miraculous consignment more than she did. Dani was Clayton's first client to receive enough recognition to be asked to do something like this. If this worked out, the sky was the limit…for both of them.

Dani smiled at Clayton as she thought of the possibilities that this would open for him. "Clay, now you can go out and get some more clients. Once word spreads, everyone will want to be represented by you."

In his usual dramatic fashion, Clayton laid a hand across his chest.

"Oh my God! I wish! Then I could pay off some of these loans." He smiled. "But trust me, this commission will go a long way towards helping with that." Sighing, he sat forward. "I'm just glad that they liked your sketches. I don't think they were expecting anyone quite so young."

"Yeah, I kind of got that feeling." Dani frowned as something occurred to her. "How did they find out about me anyway?"

Clay shrugged. "They said that they had seen one of your pieces in someone's office and thought this kind of artist would work nicely for their hotel."

Dani looked at him strangely for a moment before asking, "Didn't you say that Davenport had The Madonna delivered to his office?"

"Yeah, I did." Clay's smile dropped. "You don't think he put them up to it, do you?"

Dani shook her head. "I'm pretty sure he didn't, but that's not to say that he didn't nudge them in the right direction. I'm not going to get upset about it though. Right now, I think we can both appreciate any influence that helps." Dani smiled.

"Girl, who knows. If that's the case, I hope he shows it to a whole lot of people. You'll be a tired somebody, but I'll be raking in the cash."

Laughing, Dani glanced out of the window and noticed the cab was pulling up to her house. As it stopped, she reached over and gave Clayton a hug. "You have issues Clay. I'm going to get some rest. I'll call you tomorrow." Clayton's only answer was a huge smile and a wave.

Dani threw open the door and waited patiently while the driver removed her roller bag from the trunk. Thanking the driver, she turned back and waved goodbye to Clay. He nodded and waved back as the cab pulled away.

Starting up the driveway, Dani felt a tingle between her shoulder blades. She shivered and turned around scanning the neighborhood, but no one was outside. Frowning, she turned and stared up and down the street. Since it was early afternoon, all of the children were in school and most of the adults were at work. "Must be jetlag," Dani muttered and walked into the house.

Dani barely crossed the threshold before she stopped. Someone had been in her house. Nothing looked out of place, but Dani could feel the hairs standing up on the back of her neck. She glanced back outside. The cab was gone. An overwhelming fear kept her from moving further into the house, at least not without a weapon.

Turning back towards the living room, Dani eased the front door closed and opened the hall closet. Reaching in, she grabbed the bat she kept there for emergencies. The bat shook so much in her hands, she had to wrap one on top of the other. As she walked around, she noticed a strange smell. Dani had cleaned the house before she left, but she could swear she smelled the acrid scent of male sweat. *Not Sean's scent*. It reminded her of some of the men that hung out near the corner store a few blocks away. Her knees shook as she checked room by room. The main part of the house was clear. Still, she could not shake the feeling that something was wrong.

It was not until Dani moved towards her garage/studio that her feeling of unease increased. She hit the light and looked inside the garage. All along the wall, her tools were lined up, in order by size as she preferred them. Everything looked fine at first glance, but after stepping inside, she noticed little things. Like one of her chisels was missing from its' spot on the rack. Looking down at her worktable, she saw it lying there.

Dani's thoughts raced back to her last day in the house before the trip. She remembered placing everything in its place on the rack. That only left one conclusion.

Someone had been in her house.

The faint signs of footprints tracked through the light coating of dust on her floor. The tread of the print looked like a large work boot.

Dani's heart was pounding as she moved back through to the kitchen to the living room. She placed the chain on the door, something she did not usually do during the daytime. Pacing back and forth, her mind raced as she tried to figure out what to do next. Her first instinct was to call 911, but what real proof did she have that someone had been in her house? The last thing she wanted was to sound paranoid. But what was she going to tell them? Someone came into her house and moved her tools? She thought there might be footprints on her floor. She hadn't noticed any broken windows, and the front door had still been locked up tight when she got home. They would think she was crazy.

Dani was exhausted from the trip, but she did not believe she was imagining things. More than anything, she wanted to go to sleep for a few hours, but she was afraid to close her eyes. Knowing that someone had been inside of her house, going through her things while she was not home, left her feeling violated.

Not knowing what else to do, she picked up the phone and dialed Sean's number.

"Davenport." Just the sound of Sean's voice over the line

had the power to help soothe her. Dani took a deep breath and began to speak.

"If I didn't know better, I would think you didn't have a first name," she joked. Now that she had him on the line, she started to feel like she overreacted. The last thing she wanted was to make him think she was crazy.

Dani felt better as she heard Sean's laughter come through the line. "Sorry, it's a force of habit," Sean said. "Most people in business aren't referred to by their first names anymore. Don't ask me why."

"How interesting. Well," she paused, feeling awkward, "I was…just…um, calling you to let you know that I'm…back."

Sean frowned at the phone. Dani's voice sounded strange. "Baby? Is everything okay? They still want you to do the work don't they?"

"Oh, yes. They do. It's… it's nothing."

"Dani, something's the matter. What is it? Are you okay?"

Dani sighed before answering. "I'm fine, Sean, maybe I'm going crazy, but I think someone was in my house while I was gone."

"Are you sure?" he asked in a low voice.

Letting out the breath she had been holding, Dani exhaled. "Yes. My tools have been moved in my workshop. I always leave them the same way. And I think there are foot prints from someone's work boots on my floor."

"And there was no sign that anyone broke in?" The abrupt change in Sean's tone scared her. Dani had never heard him sound this cold and hard.

"Not that I can see, but right now, I'm a little paranoid about going through the rooms again. I checked all of them when I got home, but I didn't see anything," Dani started.

"You walked through the house by yourself?" Sean yelled into the receiver. Dani flinched.

"Yes. I had my bat with me." Dani heard him cursing in the background.

"And what would a bat have done against someone with a gun!"

Dani looked in amazement at the phone. "Sean, I didn't call you for a lecture. I was just letting you know I was home."

Sean puffed several times like he was trying to calm down. "Baby, I'm sorry I yelled. But I don't want you staying there by yourself. Why don't you pack up some things and I'll come get you?"

"That's okay, really. I was going to call Tina to come pick me up. I don't want to inconvenience you."

"You are not inconveniencing me, Dani." Sean ground out. "Sweetheart, I won't be able to sleep if I'm not sure you're okay. And… if I don't sleep, everyone in my office is going to catch hell tomorrow because I'll be an evil, cranky bastard. Then people will start to quit and the next thing I know, I'll be out of business, because no one will work for me. Then instead of having the reputation of a rich playboy, I'll be known as a deadbeat jerk…and it will all be your fault."

Laughing, Dani sputtered, "All of that because I won't come home with you?"

Sean's tone changed and the smooth tenor of his voice rolled over Dani. "No baby, because you won't let me take care of you." He paused, his voice becoming softer. "I care about you Dani."

The smile on Dani's face faded as the seriousness of the situation finally sank in. Even though Tina and Clayton were her friends, she had always still felt alone. It had been so long since she had someone who truly cared about her. Someone that wanted to take care of her. *Someone that she loved.* Pushing her free hand through her hair, Dani was quiet for a moment before answering. "I care about you, too."

"Then let me take care of you."

Dani took a deep breath, unsure of how to explain her feelings. "I can't let it make me afraid, Sean. This is my home, my workshop is here…" he cut her off.

"Dani, it will only be for a few days, until everything can be checked out."

"Really, it's not necessary…," Dani said.

Sean swore under his breath. "I'll be there in ten minutes, Dani."

"What? How are you going to get here that fast?"

"I was already in the car. I started towards your house the minute you said you were home. Ten minutes, Dani."

"But –," she started, but the phone was already dead in her ear.

Dani curled up on the couch closest to the front door. She had to admit that the thought of Sean coming over made her feel safer. The past few weeks had flown past so quickly. The art show, meeting Sean, the West Coast commission…this was the busiest she had ever been.

Exactly ten minutes later, Dani heard a car pull up in the driveway. A peak through the window revealed Sean exiting his black BMW and walking towards the front door. Dani ran over and opened it before he could knock.

He immediately enfolded Dani in his arms. She smelled the soft fragrance of his cologne as she buried her face in his chest. The strength of his hands rubbing up and down her back soothed her.

She could stay in his arms forever.

"Are you okay, baby?" he whispered.

Dani nodded. "Yeah."

Sean pulled them both into the house and locked the door. He angled his strong hands on Dani's shoulders and looked into her face. "Go pack some clothes. I'm not leaving you here." Dani opened her mouth to protest, only to be cut off.

"I'm serious, Dani." His eyes were cold as he leaned down and stared her more directly in the eyes. "You can either pack something or I'll pack it for you. You're coming back with me."

Dani watched as Sean's jaw clenched. He was serious.

Nodding, Dani stepped back from him and headed towards her room to pack.

CHAPTER 24

Sean took several deep breaths to calm down. He amazed himself with the depth of his reaction to Dani's words. The thought that someone had been in here, could have been in here when she got home…

His first instinct was to smash his fist into something. At some point, he was going to have to examine the depth of his feelings for Dani.

When she walked back into the room with her repacked rolling suitcase and purse, he managed to summon a smile.

"Ready?" Sean reached out and took the bag from her when she nodded. Walking to the car, his mind raced with possibilities. There had not been any indication in the reports of anything like this happening to her before in all the years she had been living there.

So why now?

Once in the car, Sean could tell Dani was still disturbed by what happened. Reaching over, he grasped her hand. "It's going to be okay."

"Yeah…" Dani turned to look out the window. "It's just strange that someone went through all that effort to come into the house and not take anything. All they did was move things around, and leave my chisel sitting on the desk." She shook her head. "If it had been someone who had taken something, not that I really have anything someone would want to steal, I could understand that. I would definitely be pissed off, but I'd understand. But this," Dani frowned, "makes no sense. It's like someone wanted me to know that they had been there and could get in any time that they wanted."

Through their joined hands, Dani knew Sean could feel the shiver that ran through her body.

"That's what makes it so scary to me," said Dani.

They spent the rest of the ride in silence. Once they arrived at Sean's, he had Dani take her suitcase into the bedroom. He walked over to the door of his home office, his mind already working ahead. "I'll be there in a few minutes, I just need to make a quick call." Stepping inside, he closed the door behind him and pulled out his cell. He hit the one number he had set as a speed dial in his cellphone and waited.

"McKennon."

"It's Sean. I need you to check out something for me."

"What's up?"

Sean paced back and forth in the office as he spoke. "Someone broke into Dani's house."

"Dani? Danielle Knox?"

"Yes. She didn't call the police because there were no obvious signs of a break-in and nothing was missing."

"So how does she know someone was in there?"

Sean ran his hands through his hair before answering. "She said someone purposely moved her tools around in her workshop."

There was silence on the line for a moment before

McKennon responded. "You think it might be someone she knows?"

"I'm more afraid that it's someone that I know who's not happy about us being together."

It's possible. Let me check into a few things. I'm going to give you a call back."

"Sure." Sean was about to hang up when he heard McKennon calling to him. "Is she going to be staying with you? I don't want to take a chance that she walks in on anyone while they're checking the place out."

Yes. She's going to be with me."

"Won't that cramp your style?" Sean rolled his eyes as he heard the laughter in McKennon's voice.

"No, not at all," he said, realizing that style cramping is exactly what would be happening. The time he spent in Italy had just increased his longing to be with her. It was a novel experience for him.

Even before taking over the company after his parent's death, women had been after him. His looks were a factor in it, but mostly, they were attracted to the size of his bank account. With Dani, he realized that none of that made a difference. Their attraction was primal, the real woman in Dani calling to the real man in Sean.

CHAPTER 25

*D*ani felt strange unpacking her things and placing them in Sean's empty dresser drawers. She was nearly finished when he walked back into the room. For the first time since they had started dating, Dani was unsure about things between them. It was one thing to spend time together occasionally, but it was another to move in for an extended time. She had always prided herself on her independence and being able to make decisions on her own.

Not knowing what else to say, Dani turned to him. "I'll try to stay out of your way as much as possible. I still say you could have just let me stay over at Tina's place, she has an extra ..."

"No." That one word, although spoken quietly, told her a lot about him. This Sean ran a major corporation. He gave orders and expected them to be followed.

Dani frowned. "Sean, we both know I can't stay here indefinitely and at some point I have to go back home and finish my sculptures. Not to mention the project on the West Coast."

Sean walked towards her not saying a word. As they faced

each other, he stopped and picked up her hands and brought them to his lips, kissing each one. "You can stay here as long as you need. We'll find a place for you to work. Someplace close by."

"But Sean-," Sean stopped her from arguing by covering her lips with his own. He missed her. Missed her taste, her softness. With Dani, he could see a future, a family.

"Open up for me baby," he whispered, wanting to reaffirm his feelings. Dani parted her lips, and Sean dived in to taste her. Her eyes drifted closed as her soft moans increased his excitement. His arms wrapped around her and pulled her closer. Pressing one leg between hers, he rubbed against her core, feeling the shudders spread throughout her body. She pulled away from him panting, attempting to catch her breath. When she opened her eyes, he could see her lips parting.

"No arguing," he whispered. Dipping his head, he sucked gently at the side of her neck savoring the sweet taste of her skin.

Sean's hands played across her skin. He loved the sweetness and essence that was purely hers. Sean grabbed her hips, pulling her close.

Dani's hands slipped around his neck as she ground against him. Wherever his hands caressed her, she burned. This man had the power to make her lose control and throw all caution to the wind.

Sean broke the kiss long enough to ease back and unbutton his shirt. Grabbing her hands, he placed them on his chest. "Touch me," he whispered.

Dani ran her hands over the muscles of his chest, delighting in the feel of the soft hairs that covered his chest. Each caress of her fingers across his skin was agony. Slowly, he pulled the clothes from her body, starving for the feel Dani's skin against his. He stepped back long enough to remove his clothes. Light streaming from the windows bathed Dani in a golden glow. Sean stepped forward and enfolded her body, lifting her gently and moving towards the bed. He stepped back and drank in the sight of her in his bed.

Dani loved the fact that Sean stayed in shape. The definition of the muscles in his body made her long to have his arms around her. He made her feel safe and secure.

Leaning over her, Sean claimed her lips again. Sean trailed kisses down her neck until he reached her breasts, taking one nipple deep into his mouth. No other woman affected him this way. All he could think of was giving her pleasure, binding her closer to him with each touch.

He stopped for a moment and looked down into Dani's eyes. This was more. More than what he imagined he would discover when he began hunting for someone to have his child. Dani was his other half. The one person who made him complete. With that acceptance, Sean hungrily took possession of Dani's lips again.

"I can't wait anymore, baby," Sean muttered, spreading Dani's legs and joining with her. His eyes closed as Dani's body softened to accept him, linking them together.

"Did I hurt you?" he rasped, trying his best to hold on to his slim thread of control. Shaking her head, Dani pulled his head back down for a kiss, just as voracious as Sean. Both of them were out of control. The two weeks apart seemed like forever.

Sean accepted that he never wanted to be separated from Dani again. He showed Dani his feelings the only way he knew how. Her soft cries were music to his ears, pushing him to make her lose complete control. He wanted it all from her.

Her heart, her soul, her...love.

Sean tried to remove every thought Dani ever had of another man. He wanted to consume her every thought.

Brand her. Somehow, in just a few days, Dani had come to mean more to him than any woman he had ever dated.

"Oh god, Sean," she gasped. Sean gritted his teeth and tried to hold on while Dani convulsed around him.

"Dani!" He pressed deep inside her and held himself there, filling her with the very essence of himself.

"Stay with me," Sean whispered.

He gently stroked his hand along the side of her face. "No more arguing about it okay?"

Dani nodded, feeling that they some deeper level of understanding. Gazing into the deep green of his eyes, she began to understand how much she was starting to care for this man. If she was not falling in love with him before, she was now. Dani snuggled deeper into his embrace and fell into a deep, contented sleep.

CHAPTER 26

*D*ani's eyes snapped open as she awoke the next morning, her body shuddering on the verge of a release. Her eyes flew open as she tipped over the edge, screaming. A quick glance revealed Sean kneeling between her legs with a devilish smile.

"Morning," he murmured, kissing his way up her body. He spread her legs and slid inside her.

"I like waking up this way," he groaned as he slid inside her. "I could get used to this."

Dani placed her hands on his back, delighting in the ripple of muscles flexing beneath her hands, loving the feel of him. He was sexy and attentive. Such a devastating combination. Every stroke pushed her higher, brought her closer to release.

"So could I," she whispered.

Sean reached down, lifted her hips, and began thrusting in long, hard strokes. She tightened her around him, throwing off his rhythm.

He groaned. "Two can play that game." Her body began shaking as she felt another orgasm begin to roll over her.

"Sean, I – oh god, Sean -,"

"Let it go baby, let it go," he panted, increasing the speed of his strokes.

Dani's body soared. From a distance, she heard him groaning above her. He slammed into her and came deep inside her, triggering another orgasm. She was surprised when he did not move immediately to the side. Instead he lowered his body to hers, wrapping his arms around her, holding her tight.

As his breathing returned to normal, Sean realized holding Dani in his arms fulfilled him more than anything else he could imagine. She was not impressed by who he was, or what he had. She just wanted him. He eased his body over to the side, bringing Dani with him. He kissed her gently on the lips and looked deep into her eyes. Smiling at him, Dani kissed him back.

In that moment, he had a revelation. Dani's smile was the first thing he wanted to see in the morning and the last thing he wanted to see at night. His great plan had backfired. He never expected this to happen.

He had fallen in love with her.

"I think I'm going to take the day off today," he said, stroking his hand up and down her arm. Sean could tell Dani liked the idea by the way her eyes flared, but then her expression closed off. She pulled back a little and started to sit up. "You don't have to do that, I'll be fine…" Sean sat up in alarm as Dani paled and grabbed her mouth. "Dani?"

Tossing the covers aside, Dani ran for the bathroom with Sean only steps behind her. By the time he stood in the doorway, she was curved over the toilet, heaving. Easing to his knees beside Dani, he placed one arm around her and used the other to hold her hair away from her face. Sean lost track of how long they stayed that way as he stroked her forehead, hating the thought of her being sick. When it was finally over, he helped her stand so Dani could rinse her mouth and carried her back to bed. He was scared to hope that she was pregnant. As much as he wanted it, he did not want to jinx it. There were so some many other things it could be – stomach flu, food poisoning….

He felt helpless as he watched her curl into a ball. "Dani, I think you should go to the doctor."

She shook her head. "Don't overreact, Sean. It's probably just something I ate."

"Still, Dani," he sat on the edge of the bed causing her to roll towards him. "It's better to have it checked out."

Dani's hand slammed down over her mouth again, and she pushed him out of the way. Within seconds, she was back on her knees in front of the toilet. Sean stood and watched her for a moment, feeling completely helpless.

"That's it. You're going." Sean resembled a drill sergeant as he marched back into the bedroom and threw on some clothes.

AN HOUR LATER, Sean sat in the chair beside Dani's hospital bed. He had bullied Dani into her clothes and brought her in to be examined. She had protested the entire time, but all Sean could think of was how someone had broken into her house. What if someone put something in her food? Or left something around that made her sick? Now that he had finally come to grips with how he felt about her, he was not going to lose her.

Sean glanced over to where Dani lay sleeping, her stomach finally calm. Their hands were entwined on the side of the bed. He had not moved from her side since they had arrived. He turned at the sound of the curtain sliding back to reveal the doctor, a black woman somewhere in her mid-thirties, staring down at her chart. Dani's eyes fluttered open. Sean tensed for a moment until the doctor smiled.

"Congratulations!"

Dani frowned at the doctor and stared in disbelief. "What?"

"You're going to have a baby. By my guess, I'd say you're, oh, close to six weeks along. I'm going to prescribe some vitamins for you. You'll need to schedule an appointment with your OB/GYN as soon as possible."

Both of them looked at each other in disbelief. Dani had gotten pregnant their first night together.

CHAPTER 27

*D*ani was silent on the ride back to Sean's house. Her mind was spinning. Pregnant? She was amazed. Without realizing what she was doing, her hand had been steadily rubbing her stomach. Somehow, she had never expected to have children. Then the fear set in.

What if she couldn't hold it to full term?

What if something went wrong?

She took a quick peek at Sean while he drove. She wanted to say something but had no clue where to begin. The last thing she wanted was Sean thinking she planned this. Turning back around, she stared out of the window for the rest of the ride to his house.

Once inside, Dani sat on the couch, resting her head against the back. It was going to take a while for her to come to grips with their new situation. Biting her lip, she watched Sean walk over to the window and stare outside. He had not said anything since they left the hospital, and that scared her. He was closed to her, no emotion, no words. Nothing.

"Um, Sean?"

Sean turned to her, his face completely blank. Her heart

110

dropped at the look on his face. "I just want you to know that I don't expect anything from you." She shook her head. "I honestly never thought that this would happen, not with my past medical history. I can understand if you don't want any children right now, I mean, we haven't been seeing each other that long – I can support the baby perfectly fine without you if that's what you want...," Dani stopped speaking as Sean walked towards her and sat down.

His arms wrapped around Dani and he pulled her close. Tears formed in her eyes as Sean began to speak to her in hushed tones. "Shh. I'm not going anywhere Dani." His lips captured hers in a deep kiss. "I want this baby, and I want you," he whispered. "We're in this together. I want you – both of you – here with me." More tears fell as he reached out and caressed her stomach. Sean's touch burned through her clothes and seemed to brand her. "I want to watch you grow round with my child inside you." Sean's voice grew hoarse. "I want us to raise this child together."

Grabbing her face between his hands, he lowered his lips to hers. The kiss was sweet and gentle, unlike anything they had shared before. Dani's heart raced at his words. She sat back and struggled to pull herself together enough to speak. "Wait a minute. You want me to move in with you? Won't that cramp your style?"

He smiled at her and tugged her closer. "Not as much as you marrying me will."

"You want me to marry you?" Dani screeched.

Nodding, he kissed her again. She frowned. "Sean, I'm not expecting you to marry me because of the baby. This isn't the dark ages. People raise children apart all the time...," she started.

Sean's expression darkened as he shook his head. "Not my child." Chills raced through her body as his hands eased under her top to caress her back, then back again to rub the lacy undersides of her bra. "And not you." His thumbs lightly grazed across her nipples.

Dani shook her head to clear it. "Sean, we barely know each other."

Heat pooled between her legs as he pinched her nipples. He shook his head and pulled her blouse over her head. One hand eased down and unfastened her pants, his fingers searching until they reached her center to find her wet and welcoming.

Dani whimpered when he removed his hand, watching as he drew back to peel her jeans and underwear down. By the time he removed his shirt and pants, she was more than ready for him. Her mouth went dry at the sight of his toned body with its slight dusting of hair. He covered her body, spreading her legs to drive deep inside her. She gasped as he pushed against her womb.

This time there was no foreplay, but she did not need it. Sean grabbed her legs and pulled them over his shoulder without stopping. This new angle pulled him even deeper.

"Marry me, Dani," he grunted as he moved inside her.

"We can't!" she gasped, closing her eyes.

"Yes, we can, Dani. We can do whatever we want, baby."

Dani wanted to scream out in frustration. Sean was doing just enough to keep her on edge. Opening her eyes, she looked into his face and wanted to scream in frustration. She was so close.

"Sean, please!" She used her vaginal muscles to clamp down on him in the hopes that he would give her that extra bit that would send her over the edge.

Sean grabbed her legs and held her down, then proceeded to drive her crazy by moving even slower.

"Tell me what I want to hear and I'll give you what you want, Dani." He smiled down at her. "Or better yet, I can stop."

Her eyes snapped to his in disbelief. "You wouldn't!"

Smiling, he stared down at her and slowly eased himself out, his eyes watching her expression every inch of the way.

He held her down to keep her from trying to pull him back down.

"Sean!"

"Tell me, Dani," he panted. It was agony to stop, but he had to prove his point. He wanted her answer. And that answer had to be yes.

Dani wanted to scream in frustration. "Yes, damn it! Yes!"

"Good girl," he said, slipping back inside her and moving faster. Dani's body clenched as her climax rushed over her. From a distance, she heard Sean groaning above her as he poured himself deep inside her.

He leaned over her, resting his weight on his arms. Kissing her, he slowly withdrew from her body and stood. He scooped her up in his arms and carried her towards the bedroom.

THE NEXT MORNING, Dani woke up late and alone. She vaguely remembered Sean waking her up and kissing her goodbye, saying that he had to go the office early. It felt strange waking up alone in his bed, in his house. Things had moved so fast between them. Too fast. If someone had told her six weeks ago that she was going to meet Sean and wind up married to him and pregnant with his child, she would have told them to have their head examined. Instead, here she was, as well as commissioned for a sculpture that would make her career.

Dani shivered as she thought about how perfect things were.

Too perfect.

CHAPTER 28

Sean was engrossed in looking over the papers for a possible merger when his assistant buzzed him. "Yes?"

"Mr. Davenport, Mr. McKennon is here to see you."

"Send him in." Sean sat back in his chair, schooling his features to conceal the anxiety he was feeling. He hoped McKennon had been able to find something to put his mind at ease.

McKennon walked in and reclined in one of the chairs in front of Sean's desk. "I see you're looking well rested," McKennon said, smiling. "It's not like you to take off a day. I was surprised to hear you didn't come in."

Shrugging, Sean allowed himself to smile. "I had a slight emergency yesterday."

McKennon began to look intrigued. "What kind of emergency?" McKennon's voice was calm, but Sean knew he was not.

"I thought Dani had been poisoned. She woke up yesterday morning violently ill." He folded his hands on his desk. "I rushed her to the hospital, only to find out that it wasn't poison." Pausing a moment, he sat forward. "She's pregnant."

Frowning, McKennon stared at him. "You don't look too happy about that. Isn't that what you wanted?"

Sean wiped a hand over his face. The past few weeks had shown him what a selfish bastard he had become over the years, all in the name of continuing the family business. He had sacrificed everything for his cause – friends and whatever type of life he could have truly had. Now here he was, finally able to make a connection with someone else, only to know that the slightest wrong move could see it all blow up in his face.

"Yes, it is. But I don't want to hurt her. I care about her."

"You picked a fine time to think about that. Is she in love with you?"

He nodded, feeling worse by the second. Running a hand through his hair, he pushed away from his desk and turned to look out of the window over the city. "It's exactly what I wanted. But I didn't expect to feel anything. Now I can't help but be scared that she'll leave me." Sean ran his hands over his face. "It's not even about having a child anymore."

McKennon sighed. "You've got a hell of a problem on your hands and it's bigger than you thought."

Frowning, Sean turned back towards McKennon. "What do you mean?"

Sean had been so wrapped up in self-pity that he paid no notice the folder that McKennon held in his hands until he tossed it on the desk. Sean picked it up and flipped through the photographs and information that was inside. He was only half listening when McKennon started to speak.

"In a nutshell, what you're looking at is several footprints, originating in Dani's workshop. They contained fresh mud, which could have only been picked up while she was gone. It hasn't rained in weeks, and this dirt was still damp. Besides, she doesn't strike me as the type of person to keep a dirty workshop."

Shaking his head, Sean answered. "She isn't. So you found signs of the break-in?"

"Oh yeah. Whoever did it was damned good. We got a partial print from the window that I sent over to some friends in high places to see if they could make a match. That's going to take a while. Even with modern technology, a partial is still going to take some reconstructing. They may not be able to find anything, but it's worth a try." He shuffled a little in his seat. "By the way, it's funny you mentioned poison. Did Dani eat anything when she was at the house before she left?"

Sean's head shot up. "No. Why?"

"On a hunch, we checked out the food. Someone had added Arsenic to the sugar, flour... hell, in damn near every open package in the house. Sean, this wasn't some random break-in. Someone wants this girl dead."

Sean sank into his chair. "I want to know the minute you find out something. I don't care what it takes. Post guards at the house."

Nodding, McKennon rose from the chair.

McKennon's words about someone trying to kill Dani echoed in his head long after he had left. Sean sat back and tried to imagine who could possibly want to kill Dani; no one came to mind. She only had a few friends and fewer enemies. The only reason he could someone would want to harm her...was him.

CHAPTER 29

The first thing Dani did after she took a shower the next morning and settled her stomach was call Tina.

Tina's reaction when she heard Dani's voice soothed away some of the tension she had been feeling.

"Dani? Girl! Where in the hell have you been? I've told you about disappearing on me! You still messing with the Davenport guy? You musta put the swerve on him. The man can't leave you alone can he?"

Dani was laughing too hard to answer. Talking to Tina made her realize just how much she had been cut off from her friends lately. "I've missed you, Tina. I swear, we should have just closed the gallery and brought you with us."

"You're right, you should have. Clay thinks that he's the only one that can have fun. I'll show him. So where are you? Back home? Imma swing by."

"No, I'm - I'm at Sean's."

Dani waited patiently for the explosion she knew was coming. She was not disappointed. "You're what?" For the next several minutes, Dani attempted to follow the flow of Spanglish that bombarded her ear.

"It's okay, Tina. Can you come over? I need to talk. There's a lot going on right now. My head is spinning."

"He won't be mad?" Dani heard the hesitancy in Tina's voice.

She smiled. "Believe me, its fine." She gave Tina the address then sat back to wait. Relaxing, she closed her eyes and sank into a deep sleep.

Thirty minutes later, Dani jumped as the buzzer rang from the gate.

"Chica, I'm at the gate. Can you buzz me in?"

Dani frowned for a moment. Since she had always come in with Sean, she never had to open a gate. "Hold on a minute." Dani felt silly texting Sean a message to ask Sean for the code to the gate. She was in luck when he immediately responded back.

She quickly punched in the code and ran to the door to watch for Tina's car.

Dani hugged her again and laughed. It felt so good to have her friend here with her. "Come on," she said as she ushered her into the apartment. Once inside, she shut and locked the door, then turned to see Tina's expression.

"Madre de dios," she whispered, turning around in awe. "Please, tell me he has lots and lots of rich male friends."

"Not that I know of," Dani said moving forward into the room. "Come on and have a seat. I've got something I need to tell you."

Tina frowned at her and came to sit down on the couch. "What's going on, chica? It's not like you to shack up with some guy."

Crossing her legs on the couch in front of her, Dani began to smile. "First things first. How do you feel about being a godmother?"

Dani watched as Tina's face went through several contortions. When she saw the full comprehension of her question sink in, Dani smiled. "Oh. My. God. Are you saying…? You're actually..? But how?" Dani laughed as Tina slapped her forehead. "That's a dumb ass question, scratch that. I know the how, but didn't the doctor say that there was almost no chance?"

Dani nodded. "Yeah, but evidently Sean is in that negative five percent that has what it takes to get me pregnant." She paused, smiling. "So…do you want to be a godmother or not?"

"Oh, course I do!" She said, bouncing up and down on the couch. "That little bambino is going to be spoiled rotten by the time Tia Tina gets through with them!" Her expression turned serious.

"I wish your mother could be here for this sweetie. She would have loved being a grandmother. I don't know what I would have done without you and your mom when my mother passed," Tina shook her head. "My father missed her so much it was like he wasn't there. She might not be here, but I am."

Dani felt tears forming in her eyes at the thought of her mother. "You have always been like a sister to me. You are really the only family I have left." They hugged, each lost in their own memories. Tina was the first to sit back and try to pull herself together.

"But Dani, sweetie, how does Sean feel about this? I mean, it's kind of sudden for you guys, isn't it?"

Dani shrugged. "He seems to be happy about it, which leads me to my other question. Would you be my maid of honor?"

"Get outta here! He asked you to marry him! Oh my god, chica! I can't leave you alone for five minutes!"

Tina threw her arms around Dani and hugged her. When

they pulled apart, they both had tears in their eyes. "Tell me this and I'll gladly be your maid of honor. Do you love him?"

Dani smiled. "I do."

Tina's smile faded. "But does he love you?"

Dani shook her head. "I don't know. I do know he cares about me. He cared about me even before we found out about the baby."

This seemed to put Tina at ease. "Okay, tell me what else has been going on the past couple of days." Dani filled Tina in on everything that had happened from the time she had arrived home, to now finding herself the fiancé of Sean Davenport.

By the time she was finished, they had transferred to the kitchen and raided the refrigerator for fruit and cold cuts.

When Sean walked in two hours later, he heard them giggling beforc he opened the door. He smiled glad to hear Dani so happy. Throwing his jacket down on the back of the couch, he walked into the kitchen. Their eyes widened, and they burst into laughter.

"Hi Tina," Sean said before leaning down and grabbing Dani's ponytail to tilt her head back.

Sean lowered his lips to Dani's, quickly caught up in her taste. Pulling back, he smiled down at her dazed expression. "Hey, baby."

"Hey you."

Sean straightened up and loosened his tie. "Did you tell Tina the good news?"

Dani blushed and nodded. "Yes. She's going to be my maid of honor."

"Good. Do you want a large ceremony?" Leaning back against the cabinets, he watched her expression fall.

"Not really, I mean, all of my family is gone. And yours isn't around. I'd rather just have something small with just a few people."

He nodded. "Don't be surprised if we get swamped by reporters, though. They leave me alone for the most part, but they'll be all over this."

A horrified expression crossed Tina's face. "You mean I'm going to be on TV? Oh, chica, We've got to get our hair and nails done – and we have to find you the perfect dress. My girl is not going to be seen looking frumpy!" Dani's mouth fell open. "Frumpy?"

Tina instantly looked contrite. "I don't mean it in a bad way, tu es mi hermana, but if me and Clayton didn't stay on your back, you could care less about clothes."

Dani blushed again.

"Okay. Guilty as charged. But Tina, I don't want you to go crazy with it –," Dani started when Sean interrupted.

"Whatever you need, Tina, let me know."

"Whoop! You've been out-voted." Tina glanced down at her watch. "Oh, I'd better go, I've got some planning to do. Just leave everything in my hands." She stood up, gathering her things as she went to the door. "How long do I have to plan?"

Dani frowned. "Definitely before I start showing. I don't want everyone knowing about the baby yet."

Tina came over and hugged her. "I understand. I've gotta go. I have some work to do over at the studio before it gets too late."

Arm in arm, they walked Tina out to her car and watched as she drove away. Beaming, Dani turned to Sean and wrapped her arms around him. "Thank you. That meant a lot to me."

Sean held her close, rubbing his cheek against her hair.

Frowning, Dani pulled back and looked into his eyes. "I just thought about something. How have you kept the press from writing anything about us? I've been shown pictures of you before with other women."

Sean grimaced. "It helps to invest in other businesses, especially newspapers. Let's just say that in exchange for them keeping us out of the papers, I've agreed that they will be allowed to photograph me for events. Think of it this way. How often do you hear about Bono's private life? The reporters have agreed to give me the same courtesy."

Sean decided to change the subject before Dani could ask all the questions she was dying to ask. Many that he did not intend to answer.

"Come on," he said, grabbing her hand and leading her towards the kitchen. "Let's fix dinner."

That night, wrapped in his arms, Dani had trouble sleeping. She could not help believing that something would go wrong.

CHAPTER 30

Dani woke up the next morning to find herself alone in Sean's king size bed. She frowned as she realized that Sean had not even tried to wake her up for a morning quickie as he usually did.

Grabbing one of his t-shirts, she pulled it on and wandered into the kitchen. A smile came to her face as she saw the note he left on the refrigerator.

"I'll be home early. I want to take you out somewhere nice for dinner tonight."

Smiling, Dani placed the note on the counter and fixed a quick bowl of cereal. She was a little restless. She did not feel like cooking, or going back to bed. It did not take her long to figure out what it was that was missing.

Her studio. Dani missed working in her studio and taking care of herself. Since graduating from high school, she had pretty much been responsible for herself. Her head was spinning from how fast everything had been happening to her. Meeting Sean, sleeping with him and now having his child…

Sean had sounded sincere when he said he wanted to marry her, but Dani still had her reservations. She did not want the baby to be the only reason they were together, their only connection. The last thing she wanted was to become a kept woman. Staring out the window at the immaculate grounds around the house, she came to a decision. A few minutes later, she was dressed and on her way out the door.

Sean had one of his employees bring Dani's car over from her house. She quickly jumped behind the wheel and headed to her house.

Dani's spirits rose at seeing the familiar façade. Tension melted away as soon as she walked into her studio. She smiled as she looked around, found everything clean, and put away. Sean must have sent them. Dani's smiled brightly. She would have to give him an extra special "thank you" this evening.

SEAN SMILED as he let himself into the house. His assistant had been astounded when he packed up at four and told her that he was leaving for the day. Her mouth fell open in shock and stayed that way as Sean got into the elevator. Tomorrow the whole office would be buzzing about Sean leaving early. For once, he did not care. Knowing that Dani was home waiting for him, that she carried his child deep inside …he closed his eyes and let his head rest against the wall of the elevator.

CHAPTER 31

*D*ani worked for hours on a piece of marble she had sitting around before she realized that the air around her was getting cloudy. She pulled off her goggles and sniffed. The acrid scent of smoke assaulted her senses, causing her to choke.

She glanced around confused. Dani thought back to what she had done since she walked in the house. She had not cooked anything, or plugged up anything that would have caused a problem. So where was it coming from?

Staying close to the wall, she eased her way into the living room to find everything in flames. Panicking, she ran back to her workshop and tried to open the door to escape. She turned the knob and pushed, but nothing happened. All around the smoke was thickening. Dani dropped to her knees in an attempt to find fresh air. She always left the garage windows open slightly while working to help with the dust. Taking a deep breath, she got back on her feet to try to push the windows open wider. No matter how she pushed on them, she could not get them to open any further.

Coughing, she grabbed the marble she had been working on and threw it at the window but missed.

"Help! Help!" she screamed out of the window between coughs, hoping someone was home to hear her. Sliding back down the wall, she cupped her arms around her stomach protectively. The smoke closed in around her. Just before everything went black, she heard sirens coming closer.

SEAN EXPECTED Dani to be curled up on the couch in front of the television. Even though he'd left the note about dinner, she wouldn't have been expecting him to be home early today.

He stopped, frowning when he realized she wasn't on the couch. Walking into the bedroom, he realized that she was not there either. He was on the verge of checking behind the house when his cell rang.

"Davenport."

Sean froze as he heard the sense of urgency in McKennon's tone "Sean, I tried to reach you at the office. Dani's house is on fire. I wanted to let you know, but I don't think you should tell her yet in her condition…"

Every bone in Sean's body froze. "Dani's not here. I came home to find the house empty."

"Dammit! I'm on my way to the house; I'll let you know what I find out when I get there."

"The hell with that! I'll meet you there."

Sean ran from the house and cursed as he started the car. He called himself every kind of fool imaginable for not telling Dani what was going on. Sean raced over to Dani's house, amazed the police did not stop him as he broke every speeding law. He pulled up to see Dani's car in the driveway and flames rising from the roof of the living room. Most of the house was already been consumed.

Sean ran towards the house screaming her name, only to feel several sets of hands pull him back. "Dammit, let me go! She's in there!"

One of the firefighters stepped in front of him pushing on his chest. "Sir, it's too dangerous. The fire has spread too far. And with a house like this, there's honestly not too much we can do."

HIS WORDS only managed to push Sean's anger higher. "So you're saying that you won't rescue her?" He twisted in their grasp and managed to break free. He ran directly to the door of her workshop and kicked it in.

Flames shot out to try to block his way as he stepped inside. He could hear the firefighters shouting behind him as he stepped further inside.

"Dani! Dani!"

A burning ceiling beam fell near him as he moved further into the workshop. He nearly fell over her body as he turned. Dani was curled up on her side, unconscious; her arms wrapped around her stomach as if she was protecting the baby.

Sean reached down and lifted her, cradling her against him as he negotiated his way back towards the door. He was almost there when he felt someone try to take her from his arms. It took him a moment to realize that one of the firefighters had made his way inside and that another was attempting to deflect some of the flames with a hose.

He pulled back when the man tried to take Dani from him. Instead of arguing, the man just turned and pushed at his back to guide him outside. Sean almost did not realize when he cleared the doorway and stood on the lawn in front of the house. Hands pushed him towards a waiting ambulance where they directed him to lay Dani down on the waiting gurney.

"Is she going to be alright?" Sean watched as the paramedics worked feverishly over her.

"She stands a good chance," one answered. "Her pulse is strong. If she hit the floor early, there's a good chance she didn't inhale that much smoke."

Sean coughed again before responding. "She's pregnant."

The other paramedic had just slipped an oxygen mask on her when he exchanged a look with his partner. "I'm sure she's going to be fine," he said. Together they folded the legs on the gurney and began to push her inside. Sean stepped back long enough for them to move her inside.

When he attempted to step up, one of them, the first one that spoke to him, tried to stop him. "I'm sorry, sir. If you're not immediate family, we can't let you in."

"I'm her fiancé," he said. "I'm all the family she has."

The other medic nodded, and he stepped aside. He glanced up and saw McKennon running towards him across the yard. "Davenport! Is she okay?"

Sean nodded. Reaching into his pocket, he tossed his car keys to McKennon. "I don't know yet. Get someone to drive my car to the hospital."

McKennon nodded and turned to run back across the yard. The doors closed and he turned to look at Dani. Tears formed in his eyes as he watched her lying so still. Reaching out, he grasped her hand and held it all the way to the hospital.

CHAPTER 32

No matter how much Sean tried to bully the staff at the hospital, they refused to let him stay in the room with Dani while the doctor examined her. As a courtesy, the doctor agreed to talk to him about what they found after the examination. McKennon found him pacing back and forth in the waiting room, running his hands through his hair.

The expression on McKennon's face told him that whatever news he had, it was not good. They walked over to the corner of the room, away from the other people waiting for news about their loved ones, to hold their conversation.

"What is it?" Sean said, opening the conversation.

McKennon shook his head. "The arson specialist said that it looked like the fire had been started from the front of the house. From the inside. The firefighters said they found something propped up against the garage door to keep her from exiting that way. Whoever it is, they're getting bolder, Sean."

Sean wiped a hand over his face. He hated feeling helpless. It was a novel feeling not to have complete control of a situation. "What do we do now? How do I protect her?"

"It's sure as hell not going to be easy, but I've got a hunch I'm going to work on. The people in the neighborhood do not realize it, but the city recently installed cameras to try to keep the crime down in the area. I've got my team checking the video from the timeframe the firemen gave me to see if we can find anything."

Nodding, Sean was about to speak when he saw Dani's doctor step into the room looking for him. Forgetting about McKennon, he walked over to the doctor. "How is she?"

"I won't lie to you. She is an extremely lucky lady. The smoke inhalation seems to be minimal."

"And the baby?"

"The baby is fine. I would advise her to take it easy for the next few days though, just to be on the safe side. Don't let her do anything too strenuous."

Sean let go of the breath he was holding, almost light-headed with relief. "Thank you, doctor."

"You're welcome," he said smiling. "Oh, by the way. She wouldn't by chance be the sculptor Danielle Knox, would she?"

"Yes, she is," Sean said, smiling.

The doctor nodded. "I just bought one of her pieces from an art show I recently attended. I'm not usually the type to go for that sort of thing, but something about her work just called out to me."

McKennon patted Sean on the shoulder as he stepped forward, then spoke to the doctor. "I know what you mean, doc. It struck me the same way."

"She's a very talented young lady." The doctor smiled. "See if you can keep her out of trouble."

Shaking hands with the doctor, Sean nodded. "I'm doing my best. Can I see her now? When can I take her home?"

"You can go in and see her now. Once her blood tests come back, if everything shows okay, she can go home tonight."

"Perfect. Thanks again." Sean watched in silence as the doctor turned and walked down the hallway towards the nurses' station. McKennon turned to Sean. "As soon as we know something, I'll get back to you." McKennon patted Sean on the shoulder again. "Dani's going to be fine. Her and the baby."

"Yeah," Sean said, worried, "I hope so."

Dani laid in bed at Sean's the next morning, going over everything that had happened the night before. The doctor had agreed to release her to come home with Sean as long as he promised that Dani would get some rest.

It took her a moment to realize that Sean's arms were still wrapped around her, holding her close as they had been all night. Glancing at the clock, she saw that it was after nine. "Sean?" Dani turned in his arms and shook him until he woke up. "Baby, you're going to be late for work."

His eyes opened slowly. Dani felt his arms tighten around her and draw her closer. "I'm not going to work today. I'm playing hooky."

Frowning, she searched his face for signs that he was joking. "You never take off work."

Shrugging, he dropped a kiss on her shoulder. "I own the company. It's time I was able to take some time off for myself."

Smiling, Dani snuggled closer. His warmth transferred to her body, leaving her relaxed and content. His lips gently touched her forehead. If she had ever doubted that he cared about her, they were quickly fading.

When he brought her home last night, he helped Dani take a hot bath to wash away the smoke, even taking the time to wash and braid her hair. She was surprised to see that the exact brands of shampoo and other items she used now decorated the bathroom beside his things. Smiling, she realized that he must have been paying close attention those mornings he had showered at her house before leaving.

Her only moment of concern came when she thought about her clothes and sculpting materials. Not to mention, when was she was going to find the time to finish her commission?

Sean's hands running up and down the side of her body brought her thoughts back to the present. "How are you feeling?" His lips trailed down the side of her neck to her shoulder. Dani sighed at the heat that began coursing through her body.

"Good. Very good." Sean buried his hands in her hair tilted her head back to capture her lips.

"I'm glad," he whispered. "I didn't want to lose you."

Dani smiled and wrapped her arms around him. "I'm not planning on going anywhere."

He placed a kiss on her forehead and held her while she drifted off to sleep.

CHAPTER 33

Dani drifted off to sleep with a smile on her face. Sean watched her for a moment before easing from the bed. After a quick shower, he went downstairs to the kitchen and started putting together something for Dani to eat. Shaking his head at the nearly empty refrigerator, he realized he was going to have to start making sure there was enough food in the house at all times.

The doorbell pulled Sean from his reverie. He opened the door expecting to see McKennon, only to find Sabrina standing on his doorstep.

"Hi Sean," she said, strolling past him into the house before he could stop her.

"What are you doing here? Did you not understand when I told you we were through?" He snapped. Someone on the security team was going to catch hell for letting her in.

Shrugging, Sabrina strolled into the house. "I thought I'd come by and meet the new fiancé that everyone at your office is talking about. Rumor has it that she's a little accident prone." Sabrina tossed a copy of the morning's newspaper at him. Opening it, he found an article on the front page about

Dani's accident, their upcoming marriage, and her pregnancy.

Tossing it aside, Sean's expression darkened as he reached out and grabbed Sabrina by the arm. "If I find out you had anything to do with what happened to her, I will..." Sean gritted out.

"You'll what? You'll tell her the only reason you're with her in the first place?" She snatched her arm back. "I know how badly you want a family to carry on the Davenport name. I also know about the search you've had going on for the perfect person to carry your child. I have to admit that I'm surprised you're going to marry her though. She's not your usual type. Aren't you afraid of what your stodgy old business associates are going to say about you marrying a black woman?"

Sean wanted nothing more than to physically throw Sabrina out of the house. "My personal life and reasons for marrying her are no business of yours or anyone else's. Get out of here now and don't come back. Accept once and for all that there is not, and will never be anything between us."

Sean dragged Sabrina to the door and pushed her out the front door. "Stay away from us."

Sabrina glared at him before walking to her car and climbing in. The minute she pulled off, Sean walked over to the telephone and called his security company. When they answered, he said, "Sabrina Terry is to be removed from all admittance lists for all of my buildings. The next time she is admitted, whoever is on duty will be fired. Also, I want someone over here within the immediately to change the code on the gate." Not waiting for a response, he slammed down the receiver. Sean grabbed the paper and threw in the trashcan.

Dani staggered out of the room a few minutes later. Sean

walked over and wrapped his arms around her. "You shouldn't be up."

"I'm fine." She glanced around. "Was someone here? I thought I heard you arguing with someone."

Sean shook his head. "Just a call from the job. You hungry?"

Nodding, Dani started towards the kitchen. "Starving. I'll just grab some yogurt or something. There's no need for you to go through any trouble."

Sean placed his hands on her sides and guided her towards the dining table. "Sit. I'm going to fix you something. I'll have to order something in for dinner."

"Sean, you don't need to go through all this trouble."

He kissed the top of her head. "Yes, I do. It's the least I can do."

Walking into the kitchen, Sean's mind was racing.

TWO WEEKS LATER, Dani was staring in the mirror at the slight curve that was forming on the underside of her stomach. She smiled at the proof of the child growing within her. Her miracle. For so long, she thought she would never have a family. Now she not only had a baby on the way, but an attentive fiancé.

Dressed in a pair of sweatpants and a t-shirt, Dani slipped her feet into a pair of tennis shoes that Sean insisted on buying. It was taking her a while to get used to letting Sean take care of her. The more she tried to do things on her own, the more he did for her.

The only thing that disturbed her is that it looked like the commission for the West Coast hotel was going to be pushed back. Sean had pulled some strings and gotten the deadline pushed back so that she could finish it after the baby was born.

Sean had finally gone back to work, so she could sneak out and get some air. A trip to the store was in order, and she needed to stretch her legs. The organic grocery store on the corner was as far as she dared to walk by herself. The air was warm enough that she did not need a coat and the sun shining overhead gave her energy.

Dani walked into the store smiling, not paying attention to some of the people who seemed to be staring at her. Considering they had never seen her before, she could understand their curiosity. This seemed to be a rather selective community and Dani stuck out like a sore thumb. Oh well, they would get used to her.

She was reaching for a box of cereal when she recognized the woman from the restaurant walking towards her. What was her name? Oh yes. Sabrina.

"Don't we look…domestic." Sabrina sneered as she walked closer to Dani.

"Mad it's not you?" Dani asked. Sabrina's face flushed a dark red.

"Don't be too happy with your position. Sean has a notoriously short attention span when it comes to women."

Dani shrugged. "Maybe you just didn't have what it took to keep him interested."

Sabrina threw back her head and laughed, causing several of the store's patrons to turn and look at her. "Is that what you think?"

Sabrina stepped closer to Dani and began to speak in hushed tones. "Sean would have never stooped to involve himself with you if you hadn't been the only person he could find to have his child. You see, Sean has this little problem that will keep him from having children unless he finds that one person who is compatible with him. And trust me Sean has wanted a family for a long, long time." She tossed her hair over her shoulder. "So you see, all of it was an act to get you to agree to have his child. I must say, I never thought Sean would be so tenacious about it. We would have been married now if it wasn't for his obsession with a child. So don't think for one minute that he truly cares about you, because he doesn't. He only cares about the child."

It took Dani a minute to pull herself together. As much as a part of her told her that Sabrina was lying, a part of her believed it. That would explain why things moved so fast with them. But regardless of her doubts, she could not let Sabrina get to her.

Narrowing her eyes at Sabrina, she smirked. "Whether he cares about me or not, he cares about this child. And I am the mother of this child. I will be the mother of not only this one, but any others he chooses to have. I'm pretty sure he doesn't want to stop at one. And just think of how much fun we'll have making them." Dani ended on a whisper close to Sabrina's ear.

Dani had one minute to think that maybe she pushed Sabrina too far when she felt the hands around her throat. Clerks and security, two of which were pulling Sabrina away from Dani, surrounded them. Sabrina struggled against the men holding her while she screamed profanities at the top of voice.

The store manager helped Dani into his office. One advantage to living in an upscale neighborhood was the police response time. Dani had just taken a seat in the office when the police arrived to take her statement. Afterwards, when the manager asked if there was anyone she wanted to call, she hesitated. There was too much going through her mind to see Sean. She picked up the phone and dialed one of the only two people she trusted.

CHAPTER 34

Sean looked up, surprised when McKennon strode into his office unannounced. "We've got a problem."

He rose from his chair dreading the news. Lately, there was something happening every day.

"What? What's happening now?"

"Dani's friend Tina came looking for her at your place, but Dani wasn't home. Dani told her she was going to the store and come right back. Tina went to the store, but Dani was nowhere to be found. Tina became frantic because she knew Dani wouldn't have gone anywhere to stay because they were supposed to be talking over wedding plans."

Sean's heart began to pound. "Maybe she lost track of the time."

McKennon shook his head. "Evidently, Tina tried to call here to reach you, but you were in a meeting. When they heard it involved Dani, they transferred it to me. I went down to the store to check things out. Seems that a disturbance had been reported with two women in the store. One had tried to choke the other." McKennon took a deep breath.

"It was Sabrina. And the person she was trying to choke was Dani."

Sean slammed his hand on the desk. "Fuck! I should have known she'd try something else!" Placing his hands on the desk, he leaned forward and attempted to calm down. "Sabrina made a surprise visit to the house the other day. She threatened to tell Dani everything. I made sure that she was barred from the grounds of the house and changed the code to the gate."

Shaking his head, McKennon held up his hand. "That's not the worst of it. We finally identified the prints that were on the window from the break-in and picked up the guy for questioning. He said he was paid by some 'upscale' brunette to break in and spike the food."

Sean sank down in his chair in amazement. "Sabrina? I never thought she'd go that far." He looked back up at McKennon. "So she had someone set the fire, too? That crazy bitch! What did she hope to gain?"

McKennon shook his head. "She wasn't the one who set the fire."

CHAPTER 35

"Thanks for coming to pick me up, Clayton." Dani strapped herself into her seat and leaned back, closing her eyes. "I couldn't drive myself after that episode."

"No problem. I meant to pick you up anyway and show you the new space I found for your studio."

Dani grimaced. "With all the trouble going on lately, I haven't been able to work on anything. I miss it. It soothes me."

He nodded. "I know. I remember you used to sculpt every day after your mother died. The things you created! You should at least let me place them on display, even if they're not for sale. They're some of your best work."

"It's too painful to even look at them." She shook her head. "Someday I'll be able to look at them."

"They're still in the storage room on Harvard Street?"

"Yeah. I'm glad they weren't in the house. It is bad enough that I lost everything in the fire. And now with the commission being pushed back..."

Clayton's hands tightened on the steering wheel. "That

was…unfortunate. Don't get me wrong. I know he's concerned about your health, and the baby, but all of us don't have multimillion dollar companies paying our way."

Dani placed a hand on his arm. "I know, I'm sorry. I could see if Sean could help you out with the bills…"

"No. I'm afraid that won't work," Clayton muttered to himself as they pulled up to what looked like an abandoned warehouse. He turned to Dani and gave her a dazzling smile. "Come on. I'm sure you're going to love the size of it."

Dani stepped out of the car and followed Clayton over to the building. It was huge. She stepped inside and followed him several steps into the room. Looking up, she noticed several catwalks crisscrossed high above their heads. Light streamed down through broken skylight windows so high-light sections of the floor. "What did this used to be?"

Clayton shrugged. "Some factory. Not sure what they made." He turned back to her. "Come on, let's look around."

As she stepped forward, the floor seemed to buckle, and Dani jumped back. "Um. Clayton, I don't think these floors are going to be able to hold the weight of my statues."

He shrugged and took a step forward. "If they seem to be weak in spots, we can always have them shored up."

Clayton walked further into the warehouse, staying close to the edges. "We can have the skylight repaired. If you go stand under it, you can appreciate how much natural light there is for you to work by."

Taking two careful steps to the right, she tested each spot before placing her full weight on it. She was beginning to have a bad feeling.

Clayton turned back and frowned at Dani. "Honestly, Dani, I'm surprised it's held your weight this long."

Dani froze in place. "What are you talking about?"

Sighing, Clayton began speaking. "You've been in your

own little world for so long, you've never known what the rest of us have had to go through. The money to open the gallery didn't come from a bank loan sweetie. None of them wanted to give a young but promising unknown the money to start their own business. So I had to find…other methods."

"I always knew that with your talent, we'd be rich. But you had to hook up with that damned playboy. I didn't mind you guys going out…hell, just look at the potential commission that came out of him buying the Madonna. I never intended for you two to get serious."

Clayton worked his way around until he was directly in front of from Dani. "And that's where the problems began. Now you're listening to him and not to me. And the people who helped me? They want their money, Dani. All of it. And there's only one way I can think of getting it for them." He stopped in front of Dani.

"What are you going to do?"

"Since you don't seem to want to move into the appropriate position, I'm going to have to help you."

Tears formed in her eyes. "Sean would have given you the money. You were my friend, like family to me." Dani tried to slide to the right. "If you want me dead, why didn't you just shoot me?"

Clayton shrugged. "Too easy to trace bullets. If you had died in the fire, we wouldn't be going through all this now. I could have collected the insurance money. Besides, with you dead, your sculptures will be worth more than your boyfriend would be willing to come up with. I'll have enough to pay off the money and get myself back on my feet."

Dani froze. Clayton had set the fire. She slowly twisted her foot to the side and tested the floor the her right before easing the rest of her body into the area. She breathed a sigh of relief when it held her weight.

Clayton saw her trying to escape and smiled. "Nice move. But this place has had termites for years." His voice was so unemotional and cold; he sounded like a complete stranger. "You'll fall eventually."

CHAPTER 36

Sean jumped out of the car before McKennon came to a complete stop. Several police cars screeched to a halt behind them as he ran for the door of the warehouse. Tearing open the door, his heart was in his throat. He could only watch as Dani tried to move to avoid Clayton as he lunged at her.

He started forward and watched, helpless, as Dani fell through the wooden floor. "NOOOOOO!" Sean screamed, turning to run at Clayton. Arms closed around him from behind, keeping Sean from running across the floor to Dani.

"You can't! The whole damn floor will collapse! She's not dead! Look Sean! She's still holding on!" Sean tried to shake loose only to have McKennon grab his arm and pull him back again. He could just barely make out her hands trying to hold onto the wood. The police had spread out along the main part of the doorway, guns trained on Clayton.

Sean turned back to Clayton, furious. "Why?" he yelled. "You and Tina were the only family she had left. Why would you do this to her?"

Clayton turned to him, his expression torn. "I needed money, Davenport. A lot of money."

McKennon began to speak in Sean's ear. "They've found a basement entrance. They should be directly under her any minute. Keep him talking."

Breathing deeply, Sean asked, "Why didn't you just come to me for the money?"

"Ha! Really? I was just going to stroll up to you and ask for a couple hundred thousand? You were screwing her, not me." Clayton looked around and the police surrounding him. "It's too late now anyway."

Before anyone could move, Clayton stepped forward and kicked at Dani's hands. The sound of gunfire echoed around him as bullets slammed into Clayton's body. Sean's heart dropped into his stomach as he watched Dani's hands disappear over the edge.

Sean's heart felt like it was ripped from his chest. He could not breathe. Everything kept churning his head until he heard someone yelling from below, "We've got her!"

Gasping, he turned around, he ran outside. He saw a group of policemen walking from the back of the building to where another group of officers stood waiting. When the man holding Dani exited the building, Sean ran forward and took her from him. Tears filled Sean's eyes as he felt Dani's arms wrap around his neck and pull him close.

Her body jerked in his arms as she began crying.

CHAPTER 37

*D*ani lay in the hospital bed and thought about all that happened in the past few weeks. Tina came up to the hospital every day to see her. Sean usually showed up in the evenings just in time for Tina to leave. The doctor had insisted that she remain in the hospital for at least a week to ensure that the stress did not affect the baby. To make sure, he sedated her for the first couple of days to make sure that she rested.

Today, the hospital she was discharging her and she could go home. Wherever that was. Her home, her real home, burned to the ground. The only place that felt like home was Sean's house, and she was undecided about whether or not she wanted to go back there.

As she contemplated her future, Sean and Tina walked in at the same time. Tina for once, had dressed down, the pink coatdress making her look years younger. Sean had dressed casually as well. A wrinkled polo shirt and a pair of beat up jeans hugged all the curves of his body. Dressed like this, he could probably walk down the street without anyone identifying him. Her heart dropped at his haggard expression. He looked as though he had lost weight, and there were dark circles under his eyes.

Tina walked over and gave her a hug. "Hey, Chica. How you doing?"

"Ready to get out of here." Dani's eyes flipped from Sean back to Tina. "I'm going home with you, right?"

Glancing over her shoulder at Sean, Tina cleared her throat. "Yeah, if that's what you really want."

Sean stepped forward and sat on the edge of the bed. Gently, he lifted Dani's hand and held it to his lips. Dani noticed that he liked to hold hands – to hold and touch her – whenever he was close. She thought that maybe it was because of his parents. She had always gotten the feeling that they were not very affectionate.

"I want you to come home with me."

Sean's fingers stroked over the palm of her hand sending shivers throughout her body. "I don't think that's a good idea, Sean."

"I know," his voice caught. "I know that you don't believe I truly care for you. Listen to me now."

"When…," he closed his eyes and swallowed against the lump in his throat. "When I first met you, it wasn't by accident. Everything had been planned." Sean drew a deep breath and put his head down. "For us to meet…everything. I thought that I could convince you to have my child and give it up. Then something happened. The more I was with you… the more I was with you…the more I wanted to be with you." Sean looked up at Dani, his eyes bright with unshed tears. "Thanks to you, my life stopped being about work and the next deal and became about building something with you."

Dani could see the moisture that had pooled in his eyes, threatening to fall.

"Thanks to you, I finally understand what it means to love someone and to be loved. I want to take you home and watch my child grow inside you. I want us to have something I never had. A family."

Dani could not understand why everything around her was blurry until she realized that her eyes had filled with tears.

"I want to Sean, I do. But I need time," she turned to Tina. "I'm ready to go as soon as I get dressed." Tina shot Sean a quick look then left the room.

"Give me another chance, please?" Sean begged.

Dani closed her eyes against the tears that threatened to fall. "I can't," she whispered, watching Sean's face pale. "I can't go home with you knowing that everything was a lie. That everything could still be a lie. I was nothing to you but a means to an end, and almost died because of it." She placed her hand over her stomach, covering the precious life growing inside her.

"I will never stop you from seeing our child. But I can't believe that you truly care for me."

Sean stood in silence. He realized his actions had cost him the most important thing in his life. The woman he loved and his child. Not to mention, the chance to have more children with her – to have a real family.

He nodded slowly and turned to leave the room. He was lost in thought as he walked down the hallway and out of doors of the hospital.

CHAPTER 38

Dani admired herself in the mirror in her room in Tina's townhouse. Four months had passed since the incident with Clayton. In spite of everything he had done, they had done their best to give him a decent funeral.

She was ready to begin work on her West Coast commission as soon as the baby was born. The gallery had been closed and the work previously stored there had been moved to the warehouse with the Dani's other sculptures. Tina was working with her to schedule a showing of all of the sculptures through another gallery.

Tonight, all her sculptures would be on display for the first time. With over 15 works of various sizes to display, it took a while to find a space large enough for the show.

Dani smoothed her beige gown over her baby bump. The same woman who designed the black dress she wore when she met Sean designed it for simplicity and comfort. The material was a soft silk that felt sexy against her skin. She wondered how their child would look and hoped he would have their father's beautiful green eyes.

It seemed like forever since she had seen him.

For the first few months, Sean had called every day. Each conversation was torture. Every time she got off the phone, she cried, wanting to run back to him, but not trusting her own judgment. When she stopped answering his calls, he started calling Tina to find out information. Tina mentioned that Sean had been silent for the past two weeks.

A lump formed in her throat when she thought about never seeing him again.

So…that was it. It was over. She took a deep breath to pull herself together.

Grabbing her shawl and purse from the bed, she slipped her feet into the comfortable flats Tina located for her. Tina did her makeup and hair earlier, so she would be ready to go on time.

Dani and Tina arrived fashionably late – Tina's idea, not Dani's.

The owner of the gallery, James Peterson, a tall, handsome African American man whose gallery was firmly established, greeted both of them at the door. Tina with a glass of champagne, Dani was a glass of sparkling apple cider.

They were both amazed at the number of people who had attended the showing. Several sold signs already hung from some of her works. Peterson led them through the gallery introducing them to several people who had already purchased pieces and others who just seemed curious about her.

Dani managed to mingle graciously for about an hour before she needed to seek out somewhere quiet to sit down and rest. The sheer number of people in the gallery was overwhelming.

She wandered until she located a glass conservatory filled with plants and flowers attached to the back of the gallery. Statues peeked out from fanciful locations. Cushioned benches appeared at several locations along the stone path.

Walking over to one the less visible benches, she sat down, turning sideways to lift her feet while placing a cushion behind her back. Already, the profits from this show were enough to hold her over indefinitely.

Closing her eyes, her mind drifted for a moment. The soft tread of footsteps headed in her direction made her open her eyes and swing her feet around to the ground. Glancing up, her breath locked in her chest as she watched a tuxedoed Sean Davenport emerge from the shadows.

Her eyes drank in the sight of him. His face was thinner, and sadness showed in his eyes. His black hair was slicked back, highlighting the lines in his face.

"Hi, Dani." Sean's voice was husky.

"Hi," she whispered. Her hand automatically began rubbing her stomach. Sean's glanced at her and became sadder.

He cleared his throat. "Looks like things are working out for you. Everyone loves your work. But I knew they would."

Dani stared at her hands, where she clenched her purse. "Thanks for coming out."

He stepped closer. "How – how is the baby? Have you been eating right and resting?"

She nodded. "I…," she took a deep breath. "I had a sonogram the other day."

"Is the baby okay?"

"Yes." Tears threatened to fall. "Everything's fine. It's a girl."

Sean's eyes closed as he looked down. "She will be beautiful…and loved…just like her mother."

Reaching into his jacket pocket, Sean pulled out an envelope. His fingers tightened around it before he stepped forward to give it to Dani.

"What's this?" She frowned, reaching out for the envelope.

Sean said nothing, just waited patiently for Dani to open it.

Puzzled, she laid her purse on the bench and pulled out several sheets of paper. After scanning the first few paragraphs, Dani's eyes snapped up to his.

"Sean, I don't understand."

Sean shook his head. "I couldn't think of any other way to make you understand how I feel about you." He gestured towards the papers.

In her hands were papers giving Dani sole custody of their child while naming an amount that would eliminate any worries about money.

Dani shook her head, confused. "But, I thought you wanted a child to carry on the Davenport legacy?" She frowned, then looked up at him. "Did you find someone else?"

"God, no!" Sean whispered. He knelt at Dani's feet. "None of it means anything if you're not with me. There is no one who could take your place. I don't want anyone else." Taking her hands in his, he turned them and placed a kiss on each palm.

"I'm sorry, Dani. I'm so sorry for what I did." He reached out and spread his hand across her stomach. "But I can't be sorry for meeting you." Leaning forward, he gently kissed the child nestled deep inside her. "And I will never regret our child."

Sean looked up at her, all the love he felt for her shining brightly in his green eyes. "You're the only one for me."

Dani could barely see through the tears falling from her eyes.

Reaching up to wipe her cheeks, Sean frowned. "I'm sorry, baby. I didn't mean to upset you. Stop crying, Dani, please?"

Dani leaned back and grabbed the envelope. Taking out the papers, she began tearing them into pieces.

It was Sean's turn to look confused. "Dani?"

Once she finished shredding the papers, she turned back and lifted his face to hers, kissing him.

"I love you, Sean." Taking his hands, she placed them back on the swell of her stomach. "I want you in our life."

He slid his arms around Dani and pulled her close. "Come home with me, please. It hasn't been a home since you left."

She closed her eyes and swallowed around the lump in her throat. "Yes."

Sean looked up in disbelief. "Yes?"

Dani nodded, smiling. "Yes! Take us home."

He stood and gently helped her to her feet. Pulling her close, he said, "Marry me. Build a home – a family with me."

Dani nodded again, smiling.

Sean kissed her. This kiss was a promise. A promise of a lifetime together. He picked up her purse and the envelope from the bench and handed them to Dani. Pulling out a handkerchief, he wiped the signs of tears from her face and kissed her again.

"Oh, there's one more thing." Reaching into another pocket, he held out a small box. He flipped open the lid to reveal a large marquise cut diamond ring. The platinum band was carved with intricate figures.

"I had just picked up your ring the day that Clayton…," Sean's voice trailed off as he recalled how close he came to losing Dani. "I've been walking around with it in my pocket every day in the hopes that I could convince you to come back to me."

She stared speechless as he slipped the ring on her finger. "Now we can go home."

Hand in hand, they left the conservatory and headed back to the gallery. Both of them were smiling broadly. To Dani's surprise, everyone began to cheer. She looked at Sean as he began blushing.

"I asked them to wish me luck."

Dani laughed as Tina ran forward and gave her a hug, kissing her on the cheek. To her surprise, Tina turned and hugged Sean, too. He squeezed her hand and led her out of the gallery to a limousine waiting at the curb. A middle-aged gentleman held the door open for them, dressed in a black suit with a dark red tie.

Sean gently handed Dani inside and slid in beside her. The gentleman smiled at them and closed the door before taking his place behind the wheel.

"A limo tonight?" Dani asked, quietly.

He nodded. "If you hadn't said yes, I was going to get drunk. It wouldn't have been wise to be behind the wheel in that condition."

She giggled and snuggled into his side.

"Where to, sir?" the driver asked.

Sean stared deep into Dani's eyes before he replied.

"Home."

EPILOGUE

Two months later, Sean watched proudly as Dani walked down the aisle towards him across the sandy beach in Aruba. The weather cooperated, covering them in the Sun's warm glow, while cloudless blue skies reigned overhead. They decided to forgo the formality of a church wedding, and instead, held something small and intimate.

Aside from Tina and McKennon - who served as the maid of honor and best man - there were less than ten guests. Neither of them had wanted a large ceremony. Their families were gone. This would be a starting point for both of them.

Tears filled Sean's eyes as Dani clasped his hand and smiled brightly. The loose white dress camouflaged the few post baby pounds she struggled to lose. Sean loved them, but Dani was sensitive about the extra weight. He loved her full curves and couldn't wait to get her back to their room.

His mind kept drifting as the pastor performed the ceremony. When he realized it was his turn to recite his vows, he choked, humbled that Dani was willing to accept him after everything that had happened.

The exchange of rings calmed him. He vowed to himself to do everything in his power to keep her happy. A quick glance to the side at his baby girl in the arms of her nanny left him feeling especially blessed.

When the Reverend spoke the final words, 'And you may now kiss the bride' he pulled Dani close and poured his heart into their kiss. He pulled back to see her smile, filled with promise. "I love you," she whispered.

"I had no choice but to love you," Sean replied, smiling. "You're the only one for me."

READY FOR A SNEEK PEAK?

COMING SOON, Tina's Story

YOU AND NO OTHER

Just when you thought it was safe to go back to the gallery…

It came as no surprise that they had the entire back room of the restaurant to themselves. From what Dani told her, Sean liked his privacy. She had to admit, he had style and excellent taste. Huge windows faced west, giving them a beautiful view of the sun setting on the water.

The other chairs and tables that occupied the room had been removed. Only a large round table sat in the middle of the room, handsomely decorated with clear glass bowls filled with water and white roses. The silverware gleamed. Intricately folded napkins were placed strategically on the table in what seemed to be a careless manner, but was fully intended to seem elegant. Tina felt a little nervous. Although she had gone out with Sean and Dani before, the settings weren't this formal. *What if she did something and embarrassed Sean?*

Her brow wrinkled as she surveyed the settings, trying to remember which was the salad and meal fork like they learned in Miss Petty's etiquette class in fourth grade.

"Tina, are you okay?" Dani was concerned at the lost

expression on Tina's face. While she was always up for a challenge, tonight she seemed just a little off kilter.

"Oh, no…I'm fine. Everything is just so beautiful." She turned and noticed Sean waiting to seat her. "Sorry."

To set Tina at ease, Dani immediately engaged her in conversation about the gallery, asking her about the owner, James Peterson. That seemed to work. As Tina continued to talk, she began to relax.

The conversation with Dani distracted Tina and the fabulous settings no longer seemed so intimidating. Engrossed in talking about James and his wife, Layla, she never noticed the dark haired man being led to their table.

Chills ran down her spine as she heard a deep voice slightly behind her. "Trust you to clear half a restaurant and bring two gorgeous women to a business meeting, Sean," a deep voice rumbled. Tina turned towards the voice and froze.

Dani looked over and stiffened in shock.

Sean stood and shook the man's hand while both women sat speechless. "Dani, Tina, I'd like you both to meet…"

"Alexander Peterson," Tina whispered.

He hadn't changed. Not in any way that mattered. He still had the same sea green eyes, black hair, and tanned muscular body that she remembered. Only his featured were leaner and sharper than before.

"Danielle? Christina?" He stared at both of them amazed. "Small world."

Sean's eyes narrowed as he took in each of the women's reaction. "You all know each other?"

Tina took a quick drink of water before answering. "We all went to school together."

Alexander narrowed his eyes at her statement, but didn't say anything to the contrary. Dani continued to look between the two of them, amazed.

"I…see," Sean said as he motioned for Alexander to sit in the chair beside him. Tina could tell from his voice that he really didn't, but wasn't going to press the issue right now. She was grateful that he didn't ask any other questions. She was still in shock.

Before any of them could speak, the waiter came and took their orders, including a bottle of Chardonnay for the table. Alexander hadn't taken his eyes from Tina since he sat down. "It's funny, Sean. When you mentioned your wife Dani and that she was a sculptor, it never occurred to me that it could be the same Danielle I knew, even though she was sculpting then." He turned to his host. "How did you two meet?"

Sean grinned. "Fate. I happened to attend one of Dani's shows and met her. We've been together ever since."

Tina and Dani smiled at each other. While on the surface Sean's story was true, there was an underlying story that only a few knew. It was Dani who asked the question Tina was dying to know.

"So, Alex. What have you been up to since the last time we saw you?"

Tina watched him closely as he sat back in his chair. "I went into the military for several years. When I got out, I got a job working with a small programming company creating intelligence software. I eventually bought out the company and expanded it." He shrugged. "And here I am."

"I'm glad to see you landed on your feet," Tina said. It was difficult to make small talk when the man you had loved for almost half your life sat across the table from you like nothing had happened between them.

Alex nodded, his gaze focused on her. "I guess you could say that I was always determined."

Dani muttered, "That you were." Before taking a sip of water. Tina nearly choked at Dani's comment.

"Anyway, I'm happy for the two of you," he said, giving them a smile that didn't quite reach his eyes.

Sean nodded. "Thanks. Now, about that program…"

Tina relaxed as Alex finally turned his gaze away from her. Under the table, Dani grabbed her hand and squeezed it, making her feel better.

The last person she expected to see when she came to dinner tonight was the man she almost married.

ABOUT THE AUTHOR

Toni Jackson is an emerging author of Romantic Suspense and Fantasy. The Only One for Me is her first book. Two others, *You and No Other* and *The Kiss* will be published in early 2016.

She has always dreamed of romance and mystery. A long-time lover of mysteries, she loves nothing more than trying to figure out the culprit. As a wife and mother of three, she knows that nothing ever happens as expected and uses that concept as a central force in most of her books.

She also loves writing sword-fighting fantasy under her pseudonym, Ari Drue with two book due out soon - *Anterrian's Heir* and *City of the Seven Tribes*.

Would you like to drop a note, or maybe sign up to be a beta? Drop her a line.

www.blackprizm.com
aridrue@gmail.com